Midnight Magic

Mandy looked at the small row of stables, and then looked again, unbelieving. There, his head over the half door, was Midnight Magic himself. Mandy went over to him and put up a hand and touched his cheek. He was real, he was solid, he was warm, and he looked into her eyes with total confidence and trust.

She had to be dreaming.

She pinched herself hard on the wrist to make sure she was awake. The pinch hurt.

"It's Midnight Magic," she said. "But how can it be?"

Other Pony Stories available

Eventer's Dream
A Hoof in the Door
Ticket to Ride
Caroline Akrill

The Jinny series
Patricia Leitch

The Deceivers
Jill Maugham

Pony Quest
Rescue Team
Elizabeth Wynne

Joyce Stranger

Midnight Magic

Lions
An Imprint of HarperCollinsPublishers

Midnight Magic was first published in the U.K. in Lions in 1991

Lions is an imprint of the Children's Division of
HarperCollins Publishers Ltd
77–85 Fulham Palace Road, Hammersmith,
London W6 8JB

Copyright © Joyce Stranger-Wilson 1991

The author asserts the moral right to
be identified as the author of the work

ISBN: 0 00 694073 0

Printed in Great Britain by
HarperCollinsManufacturing Glasgow

Conditions of Sale
This book is sold subject to the condition
that it shall not, by way of trade or otherwise,
be lent, re-sold, hired out or otherwise circulated
without the publisher's prior consent in any form of
binding or cover other than that in which it is
published and without a similar condition
including this condition being imposed
on the subsequent purchaser.

One

There was a great roar in her ears from the wind and the crowd. She had no time to think of that. She only had time to concentrate on the beautiful black dome of the head in front of her, on the laid back ears, on the eager body pulsing beneath her. Go on, go on, she whispered. Go on my handsome beauty, race for it, reach for it, go on and win. She was aware of Grey Mist coming up close behind her, of the cheers and shouts of "Go on, Magic, go on," as the black stallion stretched himself and lengthened his stride.

The grey nose was losing ground now and the winning post was drawing near and the roars were ecstatic. "Magic, Magic, Magic. Mandy. Mandy. Mandy."

They yelled her name as well as his. The Gold Cup was theirs; all she had ever dreamed of . . .

"Amanda Hunt!"

The sharp voice cut into her daydream. Mandy flushed, and came tumbling back to the hot classroom and the clock whose hands seemed never to move. She hated the end of the week.

Today was not only Friday. It was Friday the 13th.

Everything had gone wrong from the moment she got out of bed. Everyone had overslept and there was a mad scramble, and she had forgotten her gym shoes. She had been scolded and criticized from the moment she arrived at school, out of breath, racing down the corridor, to cannon almost bodily into her headmistress.

By the time she had been severely scolded and told to go to the Head's study at break, she was even more late, and in trouble again. She couldn't find her maths homework book. Then she remembered she had left it on the desk in her bedroom . . .

Friday the 13th. If only she could go to bed and sleep until tomorrow. Her elder sister, Louise, who was nearly seventeen, believed that it was a very unlucky day. Up to now, though, in all the eleven years of her life, nothing bad had happened to Mandy on such a date.

By mid afternoon she was desperate, and had drifted off into a daydream, afraid that if she didn't find something really worthwhile to think about she would end up in tears.

"Amanda, what did I say?" Miss Grey continued. Her words slashed through the air, and

Mandy flushed. "You are old enough to stop daydreaming and listen. You won't do nearly as well as your sister unless you fill your head with other things besides horses."

There was a titter round the classroom. Everyone knew that Mandy was passionate about all animals, not just horses.

And if there was one thing Mandy hated more than anything else it was being compared with Louise.

By the time the afternoon dragged to its end Mandy was in a thoroughly bad mood. She cheered up as she cycled along the lanes to the stables where Beau waited for her – saddled and ready.

But from the moment she mounted Beau, she knew that the lesson was doomed as well.

She could hide her bad temper from Jane, her instructor, but not from Beau. He was a handsome grey, with the most wonderful stride, which made a canter feel like flying.

Beau had two hates: white lines on the road, and white cars. Mandy, still seething from Miss Grey's comments, forgot them both.

"Round the school, and take him over the two poles at the end, Mandy," Jane said, as she watched Mandy and Beau from the edge of the indoor area. "He's been playing up today, and I want you to settle him for me. Very gently. He's seeing ghosts again."

The ghosts, as Mandy well knew, were only birds that flew past the gap in the door, and startled the horses.

The first half hour of the lesson was spent indoors. Slowly Mandy felt the anger draining from her, but she was still unsettled. Beau felt her tenseness, and began to play up.

He held his head down, so that it felt like an enormous weight pulling on her arms, and nothing she did would persuade him to look up. He saw one of his "ghosts" as they trotted past the big doors, and danced on the spot.

Mandy clung on, knowing she was riding badly, and becoming more nervous every minute.

"Relax, Mandy. You're supposed to be enjoying yourself. You look as if you're gritting your teeth and praying for the end of the lesson," Jane said, though she had laughter in her voice and eyes.

"Try again. Sit up straight, and look ahead. Ease your hands on the reins. Beau can feel you gripping and he's used to my hands; remember he's a special ride."

Mandy loved to watch Jane ride. She seemed to be part of the horse, and every movement she made flowed. She was never frightened on a horse.

She suggested moving out to the field to start learning to jump. Mandy didn't feel ready. Today nothing felt right, and she did not want to go out to the field on Beau even though they would only jump hurdles that were little more than small logs.

She wasn't used to Beau. She wasn't ready. There was always a small needle of fear that tensed her when Jane suggested a new routine. She felt as if she didn't know enough. She hadn't wanted to start trotting. She had only just begun to learn to canter, and she was convinced she would fall off.

But Mandy was too shy to argue with her teachers. She wanted to say that she felt irritable, that Beau didn't seem to like her on his back today, that she was tired and he wasn't answering to the reins the way Dart did. She couldn't find the words though, and guided Beau out of the indoor school, through the big double doors, not bothering to dismount. There was no need.

The white Range Rover came into the yard fast and braked to a sudden stop, with a scream of tyres, only yards away from them.

Beau reared.

Mandy was completely unprepared and fell to the ground. She hit the cobbles with a thump that drove all the breath out of her, and lay there, hurting all over, wondering if she had broken every bone in her body.

The woman driver leaped out of the car, causing Beau to dance angrily. His stamping hindhoof missed Mandy's face, but came so close that she saw every hair on his leg and the sudden gleam of his shoe as it whistled past.

Jane moved swiftly, taking his reins, moving him fast away from Mandy, who struggled to sit.

Beau was thoroughly unnerved, dancing on the spot, wild hooves beating a thunder on the ground. He reared, forelegs flailing in front of Jane's face. Jane spoke to him soothingly, trying to quieten his alarm.

The woman was looking at Mandy, who was on her feet and leaning back against the door of the indoor school. Fear for Jane's safety gave her courage to speak: "Please stand quite still and don't move an inch," she said to the visitor, her voice an angry whisper.

As she said it two children exploded from the rear door of the car and ran shouting towards their mother.

Mandy dared not leave the support of the door. She was shaking almost uncontrollably, not knowing if it was with fright or due to pain. She watched in horror as Jane struggled to calm Beau. Any second she felt he would tear the reins from her grasp and bolt.

Shock and fright caused Mandy to lose her temper as she had never done before. Stupid hateful woman. It was all her fault.

"Get yourself and your awful children out of here, fast, away from the horse," she said, in a furious whisper, knowing that if she shouted Beau would surely bolt. "Walk quietly and don't run or shout. If you do, Jane might be killed. So might you. And whatever you do, don't dare start that car until she's moved the horse. You should never come fast into a yard where there are horses. Now, get out of our way, please, and quickly."

The woman stared at her, and at Beau, who was still dancing on the spot. His eyes rolled and he was sweating. He looked more like a wild horse than the quiet animal she had just been riding.

The woman spoke quietly to the children and went back to her car. Beau ceased his dance, and stood, trembling. It was some minutes before Jane relaxed and led him back to his stable.

Mandy watched the Range Rover turn, negotiate the wide drive, and stop at the gate. The woman got out and came back to talk to Jane.

Mandy felt bruised and sick. She could still see Beau's shod hoof within an inch of her face. The shoe would have cut her cheek wide open. He might have cracked her skull. She might have been dead.

She began to shiver. She wished she had no imagination. Miss Grey always said she had too much. Mandy had thought that impossible. Now she was sure life was much easier if you had none at all and couldn't visualize might-have-beens.

Jane closed the stable door and walked back across the yard.

"I'm sorry, Mandy. I daren't finish your lesson now. I'll only charge for half an hour. Are you hurt?"

"Yes. I don't think I could even mount. There isn't an inch of me that doesn't feel sore," Mandy said. She wondered if it was partly her fault, as Beau always sensed his rider's moods, and an agitated rider upset him.

Jane only allowed her most promising pupils to ride him, and only when she was sure they could handle a lively animal. It was Mandy's first ride on him and she had been overjoyed at her promotion.

"Would you like to unsaddle Beau, or would you rather I did it?"

She might feel better if she had something to do. There was no virtue in being scared of Beau. Today everything had conspired to upset him.

As Mandy walked into his stable, Beau tossed his head and gave a tug at his haynet. He looked at her sideways as if trying to work out whether to play up again. Mandy stroked his neck after she had removed his tack.

"You couldn't help it, old boy, could you?" she asked. Brown eyes turned to look into hers, and Beau rubbed his head against her shirt.

It hurt to walk, but Mandy decided nothing was broken. By the time she had put saddle and bridle away in the tack room in the place marked with his name, Jane had made coffee.

"They wanted lessons," Jane said. "That was why they came. We seem to have put them off. The woman was impossible. She said she'd never been spoken to like that before and you are a very rude little girl. The horses are obviously dangerous and quite unfit to ride and I'd no right to put a child of your age on such a vicious beast. Her children most certainly won't be coming for lessons here. And thank heaven for that. I can't imagine how they'd treat my horses."

She looked at Mandy with a worried frown.

"Are you sure you're all right? Would you like me to drive you home? It might hurt to cycle."

"I'll push my bike," Mandy said. She had stopped shivering and no longer felt sick. She knew from other falls on softer ground that she would feel far worse tomorrow than she did today. She would stiffen as well.

"I could have done with the money for lessons," Jane said. "The price of feed goes up all the time, and I ought to sell two of the horses at least. I can't bear to. But you don't want to hear my worries. I'm sorry, Mandy, that was a rotten end to the lesson. You ought to have got up on Beau again too. Next week I'll go outside first and make sure nobody is rushing into the yard at top speed. That woman needs her head examined."

Next week I'll still be too sore to ride, Mandy thought. She didn't want Jane to know how badly she was hurt. Jane had enough to worry her, and within a few days the bruising would be healing and she'd be as good as new again. No use fussing. Worse troubles at sea, her grandfather always said, if she complained.

Mandy walked home slowly, pushing her bike. She'd have a bath and borrow some of Louise's herbal bath salts. Every step reminded her of her bruises and she sighed. Friday the 13th was living up to its name.

By the time she reached home she hated everybody. Especially the woman in the white Range Rover, who deserved every horrible thing that life could offer her.

Her misery wasn't helped when, as she limped through the door, she heard Hal having his Friday row with their mother, whose voice became angrier and shriller as she spoke.

"We have told you before and we will tell you again, and again, and again, if necessary, that you are not going to have a motorbike. Now will you please leave the subject alone."

Hal was nearly eighteen. There was less than a year between him and Louise, and then the big gap between Louise and Mandy.

Hal was noisy and enormous, as tall as their father, with broader shoulders. He had the sort of temper that bubbled over like a volcano and expended itself in shouts, and then vanished in laughter. So did Louise. So did their mother.

Mandy herself had a slow brooding simmer, that rarely came to the surface, but when it did it exploded and everyone was shocked as she was usually so placid. Her father was exactly the same.

"I said no and I meant no." Her mother was at explosion point. Hal never gave up. He returned to the attack time and time again, as persistent as a dog gnawing a bone.

"Here we go again," Mandy thought. She whistled to Sim, her Welsh Terrier, but there was no sign of him. She lowered herself carefully on to the cushioned window seat, which was softer than the chairs. Giving herself up to total despondency, she stared at the garden.

It had been a dreadful end to a dreadful week.

She had extra work this weekend. An English essay had to be re-written and this time she had to write about people, not animals. "People are important, Amanda," Miss Grey had said. "Animals are not."

"Beau is important; one of the most important things in my life," Mandy thought. She had waited so anxiously to be allowed to ride him. Suppose Jane wouldn't let her ride him again? Suppose she, Mandy, was too frightened to even try to ride him again?

She thought she knew the horse well even before she was allowed to ride him. She helped whenever she could at the stables. She always visited him first, loving his bright manner and his eager head, his powerful shoulders and elegant legs, his shining mane and flowing tail.

He had a quality that made him a star among the other horses. She often groomed him, and loved him almost as much as she loved Sim.

"People are beastly and beasts are nice," Mandy thought.

She gazed at the garden, trying to forget her pain. Her father's car turned in at the gate and came to a stop beside the front door.

He was two hours early. He must be ill. She felt her inside lurch. Her busy imagination went into overdrive and she visualized herself at his death bed, with him asking her to take care of the others.

The front door slammed and her father came into the room.

She stared at him. She thought him one of the most handsome men she had ever seen with his thick fair hair, beginning to go grey, and the long dark brown eyes that she and Hal and Louise had all inherited. Strange eyes that were lifted at the outside corner, with thick dark brows in spite of his fair hair.

Louise and Hal were blonde too, but her own hair was thick and dark like her mother's and cut in a fringe as it grew so quickly and was always untidy if she wore it any other way. Louise and Hal were tall and slender, like their father in build too.

She was chunky and tended to plumpness and had to watch what she ate. She did try. With Louise for a sister she didn't want to get fat. Her mother was small, but ate very little, hating to be overweight and fighting a constant battle that Mandy seemed to have inherited.

Mandy's mother had heard the car. She came into the room, her eyes concerned. Mandy watched her mother anxiously, not wanting her to be worried. Mandy had a need to mother everything she met. By now Hal and Louise had come into the room too. Hal had completely forgotten his argument with his mother. He looked at his father, who had flopped down on the settee, looking as if someone had taken everything out of his inside and left only a rag doll without stuffing.

"John?" Sally Hunt's voice was anxious.

"They're getting rid of twenty of the staff. I've been made redundant," their father said. He spoke the words with an air of bewilderment, as if they had not been said aloud before, as if it was an idea he hadn't wanted to contemplate and now he must.

Mandy longed to rush to him and hug him and tell him not to worry, that everything would be all right, but she stayed quite still.

She couldn't understand what it meant at all, and she felt as if her world had suddenly ended. Did that mean they would be very poor, and would it be the end of her riding lessons? They were the only things that mattered in her life and the thought of losing her Friday rides was unbearable.

Two

Everyone else stood still as well. They were all staring at their father, who seemed unaware of them. He might have been alone in the room, talking to himself.

A thick black fog had descended on the house. Everything else seemed insignificant beside the thought of her father's redundancy. What if Miss Grey did hate her writing about animals? Who cared if her class laughed at her when she was caught day-dreaming?

None of those things mattered any more. Mandy felt very old, and not a child any longer. They were all being faced with immense difficulties which she barely understood. She realized that, from now on, life would be very different. What did redundancy really mean? She knew the word, and knew vaguely what it meant, but how would it affect them?

Hal jerked his head to the garden, saying "out" as plainly as if he had used the word. Mandy followed him and Louise to the den. It had been an old shed, which they'd cleaned up and whitewashed the walls. There were three deckchairs and a table and a cupboard and Granny Hunt's old rag rug on the floor. It was their own place, belonging to the three of them, and each had put up a poster as a private statement of ownership.

Louise, who liked looking round antique shops in the hope of finding a bargain, had discovered a picture of Margot Fonteyn, crouched and beautiful, bowing her head, the dying swan in *Swan Lake*.

Hal's picture was of a racing motorbike, taking a bend, leaning over, the rider leaning over too, his face invisible behind the giant helmet, the streaming road slipping away from under the speeding wheels.

Mandy's picture was of a horse. A black horse, galloping, on the downs. This was Magic, her stallion, on which she often raced to glory. Mandy looked at her picture.

She was sore and stiffening, and there was a lump in her throat and an odd feeling somewhere at the pit of her stomach. She thought of her lesson on Beau next Friday. She was conscious that the feelings she had had before when riding were now aggravated. She had been anxious before; now she was afraid.

Yet she didn't want to give up riding. What was wrong with her?

She concentrated on the black stallion. He was magnificent, so regal, a king among horses, with his lifted head and flowing mane and tail. He galloped for ever against the blue hills in the distance. The picture had the quality of a fairy legend.

Sometimes his name was Midnight and sometimes it was Magic and she rode him night after night in her dreams.

Louise picked up her sketch pad and began to draw. Her pencil scored the sheet, her eyes intent, her fair hair cascading over her shoulders. Mandy wished she had silken blonde hair instead of her thick springy black cap. Louise always drew when she was bothered. So did their mother. Mandy looked at her sister and her brother. They were very alike.

Hal was sitting on the edge of the table, his face scowling, looking as if he would like to go out and attack the whole world on his father's behalf. Mandy, feeling the same helpless anger, thought how like her father Hal was. And yet not at all like.

"It's as if someone took a ragbag of all the things our parents are and shook it up. And some of us got some things the same and some of us got different ones," Mandy thought.

Sim came bouncing through the door, his small wiry body full of his own importance, his stump tail wagging furiously. He hurled himself at Mandy. She sometimes wondered how he could live with such energy. He was a small fireball, racing everywhere, always running at top speed, always inquisitive, always sure that those he met were as delighted to see him as he was to see them. She loved him so much it hurt.

He might be the family dog but Mandy was special. She knew what Sim was thinking and she looked after him when he was ill.

She hugged him tightly now, looking at his bright eyes and prick ears, at the curly tan and black rough coat.

"Will we have any money if Daddy hasn't any work?" Mandy asked forlornly, wondering if they were all about to starve like the children in Africa.

"We'll still eat, silly," Hal said, knowing his small sister very well in some ways. He often thought she looked rather like Sim with her dark eyes and her chunky body and, when she was happy, an air of cockiness about her too.

"Why Daddy? Why us," Mandy thought, but didn't say it. It didn't seem fair at all. He worked so hard, often bringing his work home and sitting over it long after they had gone to bed. He worried about it, and worried about them too.

"And why," Mandy thought, "is Louise beautiful while I look like some kind of crossbred mongrel dog with all the wrong things come out in me like short legs and a nose that turns up, and a fat little body instead of a lovely long slender shape?"

She had once asked her mother who had looked at her thoughtfully.

"Think of being like Sim," she said. "He's perfect for a Welsh terrier, but if you showed him in a class of Borzois everyone would laugh. He's still beautiful, in his own way."

Mandy switched her thoughts away from dogs. It didn't look, now, as if she'd ever own a horse, but dogs were cheaper. A horrible thought struck her. Suppose they had so little money they had to go and live in a flat in a city and get rid of Sim? She hugged him so tightly he wriggled out of her arms and barked at her, before settling at her feet with a deep sigh, knowing nobody was going to come out and play this afternoon. The atmosphere felt quite wrong.

"What does redundancy mean?" Mandy asked. She wanted to know more than that, but didn't quite know what the real question ought to be.

"You know what it means." Hal was saying goodbye to any possible hope of a motorbike.

"No, I don't really know," Mandy said. "Daddy won't go to work. I know that. He'll have to find another job. And we won't have much money; we can't have. So Louise can't go to art school and you can't go to college and maybe you'll both have to get jobs. I can go baby-sitting and have a paper round soon," she added, realizing it would be a long time before she could leave school and help add to the family finances.

Louise sat with her arms round her knees and looked hard at Mandy.

"Look. It's family-pull-together, right? We hope, we try not to row, and we do all we can because Dad must be feeling pretty dreadful."

Mandy tried to think of something to do to show that she was part of the team.

Louise was frowning.

"We'll have to keep our rooms tidy, for when people come to see round the house."

Mandy, startled by the thought of strangers' eyes peering round her private sanctum, got up and went over to the house. A few minutes later she was clearing her cupboards and putting everything away, out of sight, where no-one could see. They wouldn't look inside cupboards, surely?

She went downstairs and walked into the sitting room, Sim following her. Her parents looked at her as if they were totally unable to think of anything to say.

She walked outside. There was still blue in the

sky and sunlight slanted across the garden in broad golden stripes. How could the sun shine when everything in their world had fallen apart? It ought to be raining with heavy grey clouds that shed tears of sympathy.

Sim picked up his ball and carried it over to Mandy and barked. She threw it for him. Her mother came out into the garden, and stood watching them.

Sally Hunt sat down on the teak seat that stood just under the kitchen window.

"Leave Daddy in peace for a bit," she said. "He's hurt . . . and shocked . . . It was so unexpected. Even though you know it happens all the time you never think it will happen to you."

"Like road accidents," Louise said. She had drifted across the lawn and Mandy wished she could move with such grace.

"It's not fair," Mandy said, suddenly reverting to being a child again. She had tried for the past hour to be adult, and it was getting difficult. She wanted to shout and rail and scream. She wanted to go and tell her father's boss just what she thought of him. She also wanted comforting because the bruises were beginning to hurt so much.

"Life's never fair. No use expecting it to be," Louise said.

"Will it make much difference?" Mandy asked.

"We need to do a lot of thinking." Her mother pushed both hands through her dark hair so that it stood on end. "We'll almost certainly have to move, to start with. Find somewhere smaller, cheaper, easier to manage . . ."

"Hal's A levels; and mine next year," Louise said, her voice forlorn. "No college? No art school?"

"There are grants for college. I don't know about art schools. Maybe you could get a scholarship. We'll have to find out. That's a bit different. But Hal won't be affected, so long as he passes his exams."

"I fell off Beau this afternoon. A silly woman came in a Range Rover and frightened him. I'm bruised all over." Mandy was hoping to make her mother think of something different. She also needed sympathy. She had never before fallen on to hard ground.

"Are you, darling? How nice."

Mandy knew she hadn't been listening, hadn't noticed at all. Louise had drifted away. No one would understand how she felt about falling off. How she felt about her lesson next week. Jane wouldn't understand at all. She was brisk and no nonsense and get on again and don't be silly.

Her mother was lost in a world of her own that Mandy could not even imagine. She picked Sim up and walked slowly out of the garden gate and down the road. Perhaps if she kept moving she wouldn't be stiff next day. Every step hurt.

Along the next lane and to the big field where the little donkey lived alone. The hedges were bright with blossom, wild flowers bloomed in the verges and there were dark blue cornflowers at the field edge.

It wasn't fair to leave the donkey all alone, Mandy thought, every time she visited. She had a carrot in her pocket and she whistled. The little animal had been at the far end of the field, but she called a delighted greeting and trotted briskly to the gate. Mandy didn't know the donkey's name but she had called her Pearl, because of the pearly grey of her coat. The black cross on her back gleamed in the sunlight.

Mandy, who was usually happy, felt a bubble of excitement rise inside her as the donkey suddenly kicked her back legs and Sim sped round her, barking. She quieted him, and leaned on the gate and watched the wind in the branches, and the thin thread of shining river that glimmered beyond the fields. She felt at peace very briefly, her worries forgotten.

Pearl rubbed her nose against Mandy's shirt, and stamped a small imperious hoof, because the carrots were so slow coming. The sky darkened and a small wind whipped against the willows.

Reality returned and the bubble of excitement burst, as if it had never been.

Sim sat and watched, his head on one side, considering. He sometimes ran into the field and chased Pearl and she kicked up her hind legs as if angry and then turned and the two stood nose to nose as if they were exchanging thoughts. "What did they have to say to one another?" Mandy wondered.

She didn't want to move. No more Pearl. Another school. No more Jane and no more Beau. No more riding lessons. Maybe she'd be able to ride when they moved.

Maybe if she was too afraid she could just not mention lessons and no one would suggest it. Maybe there'd be no money for lessons. What was the matter with her?

Perhaps they would stay near and she would be able to visit the donkey still. Pearl was comforting and fun to be with and didn't have to be ridden. She still loved Beau. It wasn't his fault that she had fallen off.

She held out the carrots on a flat hand and when they were eaten put her arms around the donkey's soft neck and buried her face in the fur, standing very still, wishing it were yesterday, wishing life went on without a break, one day after the other with nothing horrible happening.

She glanced at the little watch that Hal had given her for her birthday.

Suppertime. She supposed that would be normal. They had a cross between tea and an evening dinner, always at half past six. It was now a quarter past. Just time to get home and wash.

She didn't want to think about her father's redundancy. If she thought hard about other things then she needn't think of that. They reached the garden and Sim remembered his ball, trotted over to it, picked it up, dropped it at her feet and barked. She threw it for him, but she felt as aloof from him as her mother had from her.

Everything was going to change, and all too soon.

Three

At first nothing seemed to change. Life went on and school went on and the days passed by. Mandy's father went to work for another month, and Mandy's mother seemed to grow quieter and somehow live more inside herself.

When school ended Louise went to work at the local supermarket and Hal went back to the petrol station. Mandy's mother seemed to be distancing herself and said little to anyone.

Mandy went to the stables. She told Jane about her father losing his job and that she didn't want to ask for money for riding lessons. Nobody else remembered them. Jane, in financial trouble herself, let Mandy help with the horses, but there were no lessons. She visited Beau daily, to feed him carrots, but when Jane suggested she rode him, she pretended she was still much too sore to ride.

She woke one Saturday morning wishing that time could turn backwards. It was a grey day, a wild day with the wind keening round the house.

Everyone had gone out. Mandy crouched on the window seat, watching the rain punishing the windows. She hated the world. Nobody wanted to see their house, let alone buy it.

She jumped as the door opened.

"All alone?" her father asked.

"I thought you were out." Mandy stretched herself, and Sim, who had been inspecting her father's shoes, decided he hadn't been anywhere interesting and lay down again.

"I was. Your Gran isn't very well and I took your mother over there. Mum's worried about her."

"Is she going to die?" Gran was old, very old, nearly seventy. She didn't seem old most of the time but just sometimes she crept around as if she ached all over. She had arthritis, and that hurt a lot, Louise said.

"I shouldn't think so. She's had a bad cold and it turned to bronchitis. Summer colds always seem to be worse than winter ones. I've got a job to do. A journey to make. Like to come with me? Only it might have to be a secret. I don't want the others to know yet. Nothing might come of it."

Mandy scented a mystery. She loved mysteries and she loved secrets and was very good at keeping them, unlike Louise, who always had to tell.

"What about Sim?"

"He can come too. I'll lock up while you get your anorak. Warm trousers too. Nobody would think it was summer, and we're going to a very windy place indeed."

Mandy raced up the stairs, feeling as if everything had shifted a gear. It was exciting to be going out with her father, just the two of them. That so rarely happened.

She called to Sim. He charged to the door, barking, dancing in impatience. Once the door was opened he saw the waiting car and flew to sit beside it. The car was second only to the field in his estimation.

Mandy opened the hatchback and Sim jumped on to his rug behind the dog guard. He sat expectant, waiting for them to start, his bright eyes watching everything.

"Where are we going?" Mandy asked.

Her father grinned at her just as he had before he was made redundant. He too seemed to be excited, and Mandy, as she fastened her seat belt, thought that they were going to have a wonderful day.

"Secret," he said. "Till we get there. Want to navigate for me? We go on to the Motorway. Come off here." He jabbed at the map. "And then we make for a little village called Hensham.

Got it? We'll have to stop and look at the directions I've been given after that."

The tyres swished over the wet road, and the windscreen wipers worked overtime. For all that, Mandy felt as if the sun was shining, even though the car seemed to stagger and sway as the wind gusted.

Her father switched on the radio.

"Here is a gale warning," the announcer said.

"As if we didn't know," her father said. "It's weather to fight; wild wind and high seas, and the trees all moaning."

Jagged clouds fled across a tormented sky. Headlights glittered on wet roads, and daylight was only a rumour. There were branches down on some of the side roads, and once they left the motorway, driving became difficult. Twice they passed through floods, the water swirling high around the wheels.

"Next turning left," she said, and smiled when she saw the signpost. Hensham two miles. Hal usually navigated.

"Clever girl." Her father was impressed.

The village was tiny, its old houses set back from the narrow twisting street. A little general store and a post office broke the symmetry. Beyond the shops was a sign which read "The Horse and Garter". A black horse cantered across it, and above his head was a bright blue garter embroidered with roses, looking like a very peculiar halo.

"I've heard of the Star and Garter," her father said. "I wonder why a horse and garter. A bit daft. Hungry?"

"I could eat a horse," Mandy said.

Her father laughed.

"And the garter?" It was a long time since he had teased her.

Her father drew into the pub car park, and left Mandy in the car while he went inside.

"Room for both of us and for Sim, so long as he behaves," he said. Mandy was glad to stretch herself. She made Sim stay in the car until his lead was on and then followed her father into an oak lined room hung with mugs of every size and description.

On the bar was a model of a black horse, and round its neck was a frilly garter.

"There's a cosy little snug where you can take your lass and her dog," the landlord said. He was a small man with a bald head and a tummy that spilled out of his trousers. His cheeks wobbled when he talked. His eyes were almost black, sunk deep into his cheeks. He was not much taller than Mandy.

"I can see you like my horse," he said. "Midnight Magic, he was, and I rode him in a lot of races and won with him." He saw Mandy stare at him and laughed. "I was a little 'un once, long ago. Now, the only thing I really enjoy is eating. My wife spoils me; she's a dream of a cook."

He rubbed his tummy thoughtfully.

Mandy could not speak for a moment. A real horse called Midnight Magic. The same name as her dream horse. Had she perhaps heard of him, read about him, and dreamed the names from there? The landlord was looking at her as if he expected some answer.

"Why the garter?" Mandy asked.

"It's lucky. It's blue, you see. My wife wore it when we were married. For luck when you marry it's something old, something new, something borrowed and something blue." He laughed. "We came here soon after our honeymoon, after I'd had a bad fall and couldn't ride again."

He ran his hand lovingly over the model of the black horse.

"Couldn't think of a name for the place. It was new. The old one had burned down. The other end of the village street that was. Milly had kept her garter and I had this model of my old Midnight."

He sighed and seemed to be looking into the past.

"Friends helped us move in and one of them was a bit of a joker. He found Milly's garter which she'd tucked for some reason in with the knives and forks. He hung it round Midnight's neck. I looked at it and thought well why not call the place the Horse and Garter, and so we did."

He stroked the black model again, handling it as if it was alive.

"A beauty, isn't he? He was always magic to ride and he'd race his heart out for me. There's never been a horse like him."

"What happened to him?" Mandy asked.

The landlord looked at her, an odd look, that seemed to say things that he wasn't going to tell.

"He's still around," he said. "What would you like to drink, lass? Coke, or orange juice?"

Mandy suddenly remembered Louise's favourite drink when she went to a party.

"I'd like a St Clement's, please," she said, thinking it sounded very grown up.

"And whatever's that, when it's at home?" the landlord asked.

Mandy grinned, as her father was also looking astounded.

"It's orange juice and lemonade. 'Oranges and lemons, said the bells of St Clement's.'"

"All the best people drink it," the landlord said. "But I've never heard it called that before. It's a good name. I must put it up on the list."

Mandy ate homebaked ham and a crunchy salad, with hot garlic bread fresh from the oven. Outside the wind roared and the rain lashed down. Though it was August the day was cold. There was a log fire, and Sim stretched out on the rug and the landlord walked in and out, talking to her father about the state of the country.

She was sorry to leave the warm room and go out into the yard, where the wind blew so hard that it almost took her breath away. Sim howled, as he discovered an invisible hand trying to push him backwards.

They ran to the car and Sim leaped inside and looked at them as if they were to blame for the weather.

"Nearly there," her father said, as they turned back into the main street. "Third turning on the left after we pass the pillar box."

He navigated a tricky corner, negotiating the car through two high stone pillars into a tiny lane that twisted between high hedges.

"Looks as if this was once part of a big estate," he said. "Those pillars must have held the gate and this would be the drive to the old house. I wonder if it's still there?"

The lane twisted and turned but at last they came out into a cobbled yard, where an old cottage sat like a contented cat, crouching under huge trees that flung themselves wildly about in the storm.

"You've come," said a voice from the sheltered doorway. The leaning porch was topped by a witchhat roof. "I thought you might not. It's highwayman weather. Come in out of it and bring that wonderful little animal with you. It's years since I've seen a Welsh Terrier."

She was fighting the wind which was trying to blow the door shut in her face.

Mandy wondered why highwayman weather but was to shy to ask. The owner of the cottage looked older than her grandmother, and seemed a very daunting lady indeed.

She led the way into a room so filled with photographs of horses that there was no room left for anything else. There were model horses on the windowsill and the mantelpiece and on a shelf that ran right round the top of the walls.

Below the shelf in one corner of the room was a display cabinet, the wood beautifully carved above the door. Inside stood a horse that looked very like the pub's model of Midnight Magic and below it was an Arab horse, his body tense as if about to take off.

The old lady was watching her. Mandy turned to meet extraordinary glinting grey-green eyes that shone with a secret light. Their hostess was tall and very thin. Her patchwork skirt came down to the ground and she wore a ruffled blouse and a brilliantly coloured shawl around her shoulders. The thick glossy white hair was pushed into an untidy bun, held by a velvet bow in the centre of which shone a tiny gold horse.

The wind screeched and behind the sound Mandy thought she heard the rattle of hooves. She walked to the window. The sky was clearing and beyond the trees was a small patch of blue. The yard was bordered by fields. Opposite the window was a five barred gate and here, for a moment, Mandy saw a black horse, looking across at her with enquiring eyes.

Behind him stood three other horses, one of them a mare with a tiny foal. She drew in her breath, unable to believe her eyes.

The black horse tossed his head and was gone with a flirt of hooves and a swish of his tail. He passed behind the mares and vanished. There was a sudden shiver in the air, an echo of a roar of applause, and Mandy caught her breath. She blinked and turned her head to see the green eyes watching her.

Sim, who rarely made friends easily, was leaning against the old lady's legs. His eyes watched her face, and he half-closed them in ecstacy as she began to rub his chest.

"You've got horses," Mandy said. "The black one is beautiful."

"You saw him?" The grey eyebrows had risen and there was an odd smile on the thin lips.

"Yes. Leaning over the gate, just in front of the mares."

"That's Midnight Magic. He *is* still around, you know. He's a shy creature and very few people are privileged to see him. He comes and goes. It's a very big field."

He's still around. The landlord of the inn had said that too. With the same odd intonation. Mandy considered it, feeling a little uneasy, but her father's voice interrupted her, and the half-framed thought drifted away and was forgotten.

"My friend told me you want to sell. The place isn't on the market yet?"

"It is and it isn't; I can't cope with it any more. I don't want to leave. It's going for a cheap price to the right buyer. I'm going into a retirement home in the village."

She sighed, and walked across to the window to look out at the sodden fields.

"It's a lovely place on a bright day. I hate the thought of leaving, but I can't do the place justice any more. I need the right buyers. If I find them the cottage will be cheap. I'm worried about the horses, and my cat. The horses are at livery. I hope they will stay. It's useful income. There's Willow too; he's too old to move."

There was a soft brr, and a grey cat jumped down from the back of the settee where he had blended into the shadows. He had vivid blue eyes, and a Siamese shape.

"His mother was half Siamese. She had a love affair with a grey cat. I kept Willow. No, little dog, you don't chase cats. You sit still." Much to Mandy's astonishment, Sim, after one attempt to jump up, did sit still.

"Is the black horse a livery horse too?" Mandy asked.

"No. He belongs here. But Midnight is no trouble at all. He comes and goes of his own free will." She smiled. "I can see you love horses. Do you ride, child?"

"I'm learning," Mandy said. "I'm not very good yet. Jane . . . she's my teacher . . . says I tense up too much and then the horse knows it and plays up."

"It comes. One day the magic starts, and from then on you and the horse are one animal; fused together, bonded together like Luke at the Horse and Garter and Midnight Magic."

She looked out of the window, searching the shadows, and sighed.

"I owned Magic; I was jealous sometimes of the way they reacted to one another. Now, if I had been born fifty years later, I could have ridden in races too. When I was young women weren't allowed to be jockeys. You are all so lucky."

Mandy looked out at the racing clouds. A sudden flurry of hail raged against the window pane, and the mares retreated into shelter, the foal shadowing his mother, blending with her, so that for a moment she looked like one beast with eight legs.

"I used to ride." Mandy thought that she had never heard such a beautiful voice. "They made me give up two years ago. But they can't keep me away from horses and they can't keep horses away from me. As long as I can walk I'll be down to the stables to talk to my beauties."

Rain and wind and the stampeding hooves across the meadow formed a background to the words.

"I owned the stables but had to sell. They're good girls there, and they don't mind me coming in and out."

"I can see horses here again." The old lady seemed to have forgotten them, to be talking to herself. "And a family with a little dog settling in, to make a new life."

A log in the grate shifted and the flames flickered and fired the dark corners with glinting light.

"It's cold today. A wood fire is comforting. I pamper my old age." She smiled. "I think you would be very good owners for my cottage. I'll sell it you."

"We haven't even looked round yet," Mandy's father said.

He might as well not have spoken.

"It's very old. The ceilings are low. You'll have to learn to duck your head at the corner of the stairs."

"I'm not sure it's what we want," Mandy's father said. "It's rather small."

"You have other children?"

"Louise and Hal. He's in his last year at school. Just taken his A levels. He wants to go to college. Louise hopes to go to art school."

"Two years and the two older children will leave you and take wing, and there is only the littlest left for you. You won't need a big house then."

Mandy hadn't thought of being the only one at home but of course Louise and Hal would leave; go away to college or art school, and then take jobs. They could be married and have children of their own before she even left school. Another seven years, nearly. A lifetime away.

She saw from her father's expression that it was something he hadn't considered either. He looked startled, as if new thoughts were buzzing in his head and he wasn't sure that he liked them.

The house seemed to have been built in disjointed sections, one room leading from another in the oddest way.

The kitchen was a surprising room which had been extended so that it was vast, a family room where everyone could sit in the evening. A warm Aga dominated one corner. Huge windows looked out over the horse field. Beyond a post and rail fence the swelling river tumbled over its banks, hinting at possible floods.

Willow, who had followed them, settled himself with a deep purr on the rug, and stretched his tummy out to the heat.

"The Aga is my only means of cooking," the old lady said. "I don't like electricity and there is no gas laid on. I've always been afraid of gas. I expect you'll need to make a lot of changes."

Mandy's father looked out at the river and frowned.

"Do the fields flood in bad weather?"

"Only the fringe of the far water meadow. It never comes up to the horse field. The ground rises, though you don't notice it from here. The rain's easing. We'll go out and look around in a few minutes.

"I had the kitchen modernized, and the bathroom; the rest I left alone. It doesn't do to alter too much of the past."

The bedrooms made Mandy feel as if she had walked into a Victorian household. They all had brass bedsteads and patchwork quilts. Each room had a text over the bed, written in cross stitch on a sampler.

"Those are very old," the old lady said. "Sarah Holt was my great grandmother. I can see her sitting in the room downstairs night after night, stitching away."

Mandy looked at the tiny initials. S.H.

"They're my mum's initials," she said. "She's Sarah Hunt, only everyone calls her Sally."

"S.H. So of course you were meant to live here. What could be more appropriate than Hunts in Hunt Cottage. Besides, Midnight set his seal of approval on you."

Mandy loved the cottage and the horses in the fields. She looked out of a window set high in the roof, and saw meadows all around her, and the far away shine of water slipping through green banks. The clouds had parted, allowing a faint sun to glisten their edges with gold. The mares and foal were grazing at the far end of the field. There was no sign of the black horse.

If only they could come here to live. She felt as if she belonged here.

"This will be your room," the old lady said, as if everything was already settled. "I'll leave you most of my books. You'll need them."

She flung the door open and Mandy stared. Every inch of the walls was covered with shelving.

There were so many books. It was just like a library.

Every book was about horses.

Her father had gone downstairs again. Mandy turned to look out of the window. In the field below, standing at the gate, was the black horse, his head looking up towards her, his brown eyes glowing. The old lady was beside her.

"He's part of the village, part of its history. Born here and bred here and living on for ever."

Her father had walked out into the yard. There was a quick shift of light as if a shadow had moved, and the gate was empty.

The sun shone suddenly and brilliantly through scattering clouds. Long shadows drifted from under the trees. Mandy was sure that a darker shadow stood among them, watching.

Sim, escaping from her grasp, sat in the middle of the room and howled.

Four

Mandy stared at Sim. His unearthly howling continued and the old lady knelt down and put her arms around him and her face against his head.

She seemed to be listening intently, and as she listened, she began to murmur, soft words that were impossible for Mandy to hear. Sim quieted, but his small body trembled, and he stared with bewildered eyes up at the face that peered so intently into his.

The long thin hands stroked him gently, down his back and down his flanks, across his chest. Long soothing strokes.

"I think there may be trouble at home," the old lady said. "Sim senses it." She sighed, and moved slowly across the room. "Dogs have extra senses. They warn us of storms, and of earthquakes, long before they happen."

Trouble? Mandy's eyes darkened. Panic choked her. The old lady sensed her fear.

"Troubles come and go, child. They're part of

life. None of us can escape them. We have to learn to cope. Let's find your father. I think he has gone to look at the fields and the river."

Mandy lifted Sim, clutching him, and he licked her nose. The familiar gesture reassured her. She understood his small world. Or did she? Why had he howled?

They went through the witchhat porch and out into the yard. Mandy's father was walking towards them across the largest field and ten paces behind him walked the black horse, as if stalking him.

"It might be as well to phone home," the old lady said, as he came through the gate. The horse was watching them with bright eyes, his tail swishing.

"To phone?" John Hunt's eyes turned to look into the house.

The old lady's voice was apologetic.

"Sim was distressed. Dogs can sense things that we can't. I'd feel happier if you did ring." She looked across the fields. Though the sun shone, rain still dripped from the overhanging trees. "Will you want to move in soon? My room is ready for me, and I can go whenever I like."

Mandy's father frowned.

"I haven't decided yet."

The old lady moved briskly and opened the gate for them.

"You can ring home from the Horse and Garter."

A brilliant beautiful smile lit her face and her eyes. "The cottage is yours. I like you both and feel you would care for it as much as I do, and care for the horses. I'm not seeing any more buyers."

"I'll let you know." Mandy knew from her father's voice he had no intention of moving to the cottage. She looked at the mares and the black horse under the trees. She would have loved to move in. To have horses outside her windows by day and in the stables at night.

"I'll look forward to that. It's hard to leave at my age. It's taken a long time to make up my mind. It's a good place for a girl to grow up in. I grew up here. I never married, but there have always been children in my life. I used to teach them to ride."

She watched Mandy's father reverse the car, and waved as she closed the yard gate behind them. Mandy was aware of the horse, leaning his head on his mistress's shoulder.

"He's so beautiful," Mandy said.

"Who is?"

"The black stallion."

"I didn't see him," her father said. "I couldn't think what either of you were talking about."

"You saw the old lady and the mares and the

foal?" Mandy asked, wondering if any of them had been real. She felt as if she were dreaming.

"Of course I did." Her father was worried, and his voice was impatient. "I feel sorry for the old lady, having to leave the place she has lived in all her life. I can see why she is so anxious to sell it to us. But I don't think we could even contemplate it." He stopped talking as he waited for traffic to clear so that he could turn into the village street. "The house is too small. There's too much land. Your mother doesn't like horses."

He parked in the yard at the Horse and Garter.

"I can't believe there's anything wrong. It's ridiculous. All the same, now she's put the idea into my mind . . ." He didn't finish the sentence.

He climbed out of the car, and waited for Mandy before locking it.

"She's very persuasive. She's trying to make conditions. There would be snags about the sale, and we'd find ourselves lumbered with something we don't want and can never get rid of if we don't take care."

Her father knocked at the closed door of the inn. Luke came to it, opened it, and smiled his welcome.

"We've been looking round the old Hunt cottage," Mandy's father said. "The old lady says I need to telephone; something's wrong. I don't know why I believed her."

"Because you're not so green as you're cabbage looking," the man said, and laughed wheezily. "If Kirstie says you need to phone, you need to phone. I always trust her hunches. What made her say that, I wonder?"

"My dog howled," Mandy said.

"Ah. That's it then." Luke said it with conviction. "Kirstie knows dogs and knows horses. She isn't often wrong. Come in, come in and perhaps the little lass would like one of her St Clement's?"

Mandy sat sipping on the tapestry window seat and looked out at bright tubs of flowers dotted round a green garden. There were oak seats and tables, and a white dog lying in the sun, his legs and tail twitching as he dreamed.

"Did you like the cottage?" Luke asked, while her father went to the telephone.

"Yes. It would be nice to live with horses." It would be heaven to live with horses, Mandy thought, but didn't say it aloud.

"You ride?"

"I'm having lessons." She thought of Beau, and felt again that tremor of fear that had been growing since he threw her in the yard. The fear that something might make him shy again, that she wouldn't be able to control the shy and that next time she would have a serious injury. She could still feel the bruising. If she fell off again she knew she wouldn't be able to remount.

She watched her father put the phone down and walk towards her, his face anxious.

"Your mother's in hospital," he said. "Gran rang Louise at work this morning. She's got peritonitis; a burst appendix . . . she must have been in pain for months."

Mandy thought of her mother growing quieter and quieter, sinking into herself. Sitting bent over, holding herself. None of them had thought. None of them had noticed.

"Remember when she had flu and none of us knew?" Mandy asked. "She just quietly fainted one morning and the doctor was angry with her for trying to carry on."

"She said she had a pain," her father said. "She just took indigestion tablets and hoped it would go away. I've been too concerned about my job and our moving to bother."

And I've been living inside my own head only worrying about me, Mandy thought. Being afraid to ride. Not wanting to leave home, losing Beau. Why am I so mixed up?

She tried to think about her mother.

"Will she die?" she asked, terror darkening the day.

"They're still operating. They started at half past three. We can't see her until tomorrow at the earliest . . . why didn't I see?"

The fat man looked at them, his eyes concerned.

"What you need is a nice hot cup of tea, before you go off home. It's a long journey and there's nothing you can do tonight." He went to the door that led to an inner room and called, "Millie, we've company needing comfort. They've had bad news."

The woman who came into the room was tall and dark with a high colour. Her black hair was caught in a pony tail by a deep red velvet ribbon.

The fat man saw Mandy looking at his wife's eyes. They were exactly like Beau's.

"You can see why I married her," he said, and laughed. "Eyes like a horse, great brown eyes with long lashes. Couldn't resist them, could I? I tell her not to wear red ribbons. She doesn't kick."

Mandy's father stared at him.

Luke laughed.

"The lass ought to know," he said.

"You put red ribbons in a horse's tail to warn people it kicks," Mandy said. "Then everybody keeps clear of its hind legs."

Millie, smiling, set plates of buttered scones and currant cake in front of them, and then returned with a tray on which was a brown teapot, and chunky cream and brown coloured pottery mugs painted with horses' heads.

Luke took a scone and chewed it thoughtfully.

"So Kirstie's thinking of leaving the cottage? I suppose it's time; she must be over eighty, though you'd never guess it. She's no feeble old lady, ready to sit and knit or watch TV all day. Can't imagine her in the home, though it's a very good one." He turned to look at the model of the black horse that stood on the bar.

"Old age is sad. In her day Kirstie was a rare beauty. And what a rider!" He sighed, looking back, remembering.

"She'll teach you, lass, if you let her. She's a wonderful teacher. There's many on the showjumping circuit that owe their skill to her."

He cut himself an enormous slice of fruit cake.

"I'd have done better to marry a bad cook," he said, and grinned at Mandy. "What did you see there, lass? Your face tells me of secrets."

"Only the mares and the foal and her black horse, and Willow the cat," Mandy said.

Luke looked at his wife, who raised her eyebrows and then smiled a sudden vivid smile, as if she had just been told long-awaited news.

"Midnight Magic. He's part of Hensham. Always was," she said.

"He's no time for strangers; for those that won't fit." Luke poured himself a second cup of tea. "Eh, I miss those days," he added.

He pointed to a framed photograph on the wall and Mandy saw the man he once had been, small and wiry, a peaked cap on his head, and a black horse racing to victory beneath him.

"That was in our heyday," Luke said, becoming just a little fat man with a few grey hairs clinging to a shining head.

"Those were the days." His voice was wistful. "What would your name be, squire?"

"John Hunt. And this is Amanda . . . Mandy."

"Hunts in the Hunt Cottage. What could be more right? We'll be seeing you again, squire. Make no mistake. And I wish that good lady of yours a very quick recovery."

Millie, who had gone out of the room, came back with a packet of sandwiches and cake and two bottles of bitter lemon.

"To help on your journey. I do hope that your wife is soon well again."

Mandy's father took out his wallet. Luke put a hand on his arm and pushed it away from him.

"We never charge our friends," he said. "Safe journey, and when you come back here to live there'll always be a St Clement's ready for you."

Mandy's thoughts were spinning as they drove home. Her father said little. He was too worried. Mandy was frightened. Her mother had never been really ill before and had never needed an operation. If only they hadn't gone so far that day.

She tried to distract herself. If only they could

live in the cottage. If they had to move and leave everything they knew behind, at least there would be horses there.

She fell asleep and dreamed that she was riding Beau. They came to a tiny stream, and Jane, out of sight behind her, called out to her.

"Jump, Mandy, Jump."

Beau soared into the air and for a moment all was well. Then she was slipping, sliding, falling, falling . . .

She woke with a start, surprised to find herself still in the car, the road speeding away under their wheels.

Waking wasn't much better than sleeping. Her mother was ill and everything was going wrong. Each day seemed to bring worse news. She remembered her dream too vividly. Even her riding was suffering now. She tried to remember Beau as he really was, kind, and gentle, and so easy to ride on her good days. There had been very few of those just lately.

It was her own fault, she knew.

She had had one lesson on Dart since her fall. That had not lasted long as she was much too sore to ride.

"Try," Jane said. "Or you'll lose your nerve."

She didn't say that she had already lost it.

During that lesson Jane had scolded her for

clutching the reins too tightly. She was clamped into the saddle, holding on for her life.

"Imagine the bit in your own mouth, Mandy," Jane said. "You're hurting Dart. That's why he's edgy. He's never been like that before with you. Relax. He'll help you, but only if you help him."

Dart felt different, dancing impatiently, throwing up his head, trying to ease the bit. Try as she would, she couldn't release her grip on the reins.

"Easy on his poor mouth. It's very soft. I don't let insensitive people ride him. He's a halfway stage to Beau. You want to ride Beau again, don't you? I thought Dart would help you gain confidence. I know it was a very nasty fall, but you have to forget that."

Maybe Jane wouldn't let her ride Beau again.

She hadn't relaxed and she hadn't wanted to ride Dart in the outdoor school in case another car drove in fast and she fell off again.

She hugged Sim and stared out at the darkening sky, wishing they were home.

Five

Months later, Mandy was to look back on the next few weeks, and feel as if she had been part of a dream. Time raced, each day passing faster than the one before, with so much happening that it was hard to believe.

The days had a pattern to them. Her father was up first, calling them and then she helped prepare breakfast, so that Hal and Louise could leave for their work on time. Between them they worked out the household jobs, so that her father did the cleaning and washing, and Mandy made the beds, and tidied up and shopped, and looked after Sim.

That first week, she stayed at home while her father went to the hospital. He came home quiet, the first two days, his face worried, only saying their mother was as well as could be expected. Mandy, unable to sleep, worried in case their mother died. She couldn't bear the thought and crept downstairs to find Sim, and take him up to lie on her bed. He missed her mother and searched the house forlornly and had gone to lie that first day with his head on one of her bedroom slippers.

"He thinks she's gone for ever," Mandy said.

"Don't be daft. Dogs can't think." Hal was waiting for his A level results, and was on edge. Louise came home tired and sat and drew for hours on end. Her father never seemed to hear anything any of them said.

Mandy spent hours with Pearl and many hours helping Jane, though she did not even want to ride. Jane no longer insisted that she tried at least to take Dart from the stable to the school for other children's lessons.

She dreamed of Midnight Magic, but now he was a real horse, and not part of her imagination. Maybe she would ride him one day. Maybe she would stop being afraid. The fear was worse, and though she told herself not to be silly, that did no good at all.

Another Friday. The day dawned fine, with a hot sun that scorched out of a cloudless sky. It was hard to work, and Mandy was glad when the chores were done, and her father gone off to the hospital. Her mother was improving and they could visit her on Sunday. She might be home next week. A small bubble of happiness began to rise.

Jane had gone out for the day, to take a mare to the stallion. She wanted her new acquisition to have a foal. Mandy had promised to help with evening stables. She wished she didn't have to wait. Time passed slowly, the only sound that of the ticking clock. Mandy sat alone, hugging Sim, reading a book that Jane had lent her on stable management. One day she'd have her own horse.

She was thankful when the clock's lagging hands pointed at last to 5.30. Sim, who hated to be by himself, moaned noisily as she cycled off.

Today Mandy intended to ride again. She had been putting it off too long. She'd gain confidence once she was in the saddle. Her bruises had gone and she no longer felt sore or stiff.

It was easy to work with horses on the ground; not so easy to get onto their backs. She happily cleaned saddles, and bridles, groomed the ponies, fetched water, and filled the haynets, though Jane had to hang them up as Mandy couldn't reach.

Today would be different. Today she would conquer fear. Today she had told Jane she was going to ride. She had been saving her pocket money as she didn't want to ask her father to pay for the lessons. It might embarrass him to have to say no because they no longer had enough money.

She rested her bicycle against the old brick wall. It was covered with honeysuckle that scented the air. There was no sign of a saddled horse in the stable yard, nor of Jane.

Mandy walked slowly across the yard. There

were so few horses left. Beau huffed to her and she stroked his neck, as he looked out over the half door. No sign of any saddle or bridle. Dart, the bay, and Tempest, a Welsh cob that Mandy had ridden on many occasions, were both leaning over their half doors, eager for company. She loved the row of enquiring heads and brilliant eyes, the warm horse smell and the rustle in the straw as they moved.

But where was Lindsay, the little chestnut mare, that was only just not a pony? She was a charming little animal with wings in her hooves. Jane rode her in the local gymkhanas, often winning. She should have been in the stable next to Dart, but the door stood wide open and there was no sign of her. Surely Jane didn't intend Mandy to ride her today? Nobody but Jane ever rode Lindsay.

Mandy walked round the house, taking a short cut through the overgrown thistle starred grass. The neglected flowerbeds were thick with weeds. There was only the isolation stable round here, where sick horses were stabled. It was close to the kitchen door so that they could be kept under close supervision.

Jane's worried face looked out at Mandy.

"Mandy, I'm sorry. I can't give you a lesson today."

"Is Lindsay ill?"

"No. Yes. Not exactly. Two boys opened the field gate and then chased the horses on motorbikes. They went out on to the main road and over the fields. Dart and Tempest were OK, but Lindsay jumped a barbed wire fence. You know how nervy she is. That's why I never let anyone else ride her."

Jane pushed her hair out of her eyes. Her shirt was covered in mud.

"One of them hit her with a stick, the farmer said. He saw them, but couldn't catch them. She tangled in the wire and cut her hind legs badly and fell into the ditch. She's mud to the eyeballs and I'm waiting for the vet. I must get her clean and dry. She's shivering so much, and I need to clean these awful cuts first." She sounded desperate.

Mandy flung her jacket over the old roller that stood by the back door and walked quietly into the stable. Lindsay stood there, unrecognizable. Only her eyes and nose were clean.

"They've only just unloaded her. They had to get the firemen to pull her out. Luckily she was too terrified to play them up. She's in deep shock. The farmer gave her whisky. I don't know that that's any help."

Mandy watched as Jane balled up clumps of hay and began to rub the pony clean, hissing softly through her teeth. Mandy took some hay and rolled it, and began on the pony's other side, surprised to find that this actually worked. Soon she was very hot, but Lindsay was still shivering.

"When we've got most of the mud off her we can start using my big rough towels."

"What about kitchen paper?" Mandy asked. "I use it to dry Sim. It would take a lot, though."

"That doesn't matter. I've got six rolls; it might well make a start. This way takes for ever."

Mandy suddenly realized that Jane was very angry indeed, and having trouble in controlling herself.

"I wish we could catch the little thugs. I'd teach them a lesson. Nobody else ever seems to. I heard the bikes but they were out on the main road and I just didn't think anything of it. The field is too far from the house. I can't hear from my bedroom." She rubbed as if she were rubbing her fury away.

"The field was empty when I went to fetch them in this morning. They went out through the far gate and across the next field, so I didn't hear hooves. I rang the police and then took out the Land Rover. I'd just given up when the farmer rang to say he had them in his field."

Lindsay flicked her ears and shifted her weight from one hoof to the other. She sneezed.

"That's the first sign of life she's given. Maybe she'll be OK. But it's a terrible gash on her hind leg. I thought it would never stop bleeding. All the horses are the worse for their adventure and will have to be rested. They galloped on the hard road in front of those damned bikes. I can't use them for any lessons for at least a week."

Mandy listened, not knowing what to say. There didn't seem to be any words that would comfort Jane. She went on rubbing, thankful to see that the mud was coming off, and that the shivering was less.

"We may be able to rub her warm." Jane needed to talk. "It's taken all day to retrieve them and rescue poor Lindsay."

Mandy knew that only idiots galloped horses on hard roads. Lindsay stood with her head down, making little effort to resist them. She seemed not to care what was happening to her. Jane had positioned her so that she could tug at her haynet if she wished, but the little mare had no desire to do anything at all.

"I wish she'd fuss," Jane said. "She's much too quiet."

"Perhaps she had too much whisky and feels rotten because of it," Mandy said, without thinking too hard about her words.

"Cheer me up, do," Jane said, but she laughed as she spoke, and rubbed harder at Lindsay's neck.

"Only me," a soft voice said from outside and the mare pricked her ears.

"It's Damon, the vet," Jane said. "Lindsay adores him. He might buy her when I move."

Mandy looked up at the tall man who came into the stable, moving very quietly, talking softly as he came.

"Poor old girl, what have they done to you?" The needle had slipped in and out before the horse knew it. She turned to look at the man, and he stroked her neck gently. "That'll help. Now let's have a look at those legs."

It was time for Mandy to go home. She was already late and she should have had supper ready. She'd have to wash herself before she could cook as she was nearly as muddy as Lindsay. She wished she could have stayed to help.

"Don't worry, Mandy. She'll be all right," Jane said. "You've been a terrific help. Halved my work. Thanks."

"She'll be fine." Damon's soft voice was reassuring. "You and Jane have done a good job on her. A couple of months and nobody will know that anything was ever wrong with her."

Mandy cycled home.

She had a quick bath and changed into clean clothes before she began to prepare the food and set the table. Cold meat from last night and lettuce and tomatoes. Coleslaw and tinned potato salad. Fresh plums and cheese and biscuits.

Her father was late.

"Sorry, love," he said. "I've had problems." He helped himself to potato salad. "Your mother comes home on Wednesday. And I've just sold the house and the buyer wants to be in by the end of August."

"In three weeks?" Mandy was appalled at the sudden change in their lives. She had known they would move, but not quite so soon.

"Yes. She's the new headmistress of the comprehensive school. She's going to rent it furnished to start with as lawyers always take so long to complete the business." He sighed. "It's going to be tough moving for all of us. Now it's come to it, I wish we could stay. But this house is far too expensive and we'd have to spend most of the money I have on its mortgage. Which really wouldn't be fun for any of us."

"Why is she renting our furniture?" Mandy asked. It seemed a strange thing to do.

"She's living with her mother at present and hasn't any furniture of her own. Her mother doesn't want to move away from all her friends."

He was pouring salad cream as if he needed the whole bottle. He saw Mandy's glance, looked down at his plate, and grinned at her.

"Not thinking. I'll get fat on that, won't I? Her name's Miss Elton. She was rather worried about the timing, in case we couldn't move out, but it'll work out quite well."

"Where will we live?" Mandy asked.

"At Hunt Cottage. We're renting that furnished for a year. Miss Holt was going to have the furniture auctioned and is rather pleased that she needn't do that yet. That's why I was so long. I went to see our solicitor to get the contract for this house drawn up and then rang to ask Miss Holt if it were possible for us to move there and she seemed to think it had all been arranged already. She's really very odd."

"She's old," Mandy said, as if that explained everything. She chewed her meat thoughtfully before speaking again. "Will the horses stay?"

Her father laughed. "Yes. She's telling the people who have them at livery that we won't make any changes. They look after them in summer and only need the grazing. They're all ponies, used for hacking, and don't need schooling. In winter we look after them and simply bring them in and turn them out on fine days. She says Midnight Magic goes with the place and we'll never be able to get rid of him."

Mandy thought of the black horse in the shadows. She would have horses, but she wouldn't see Jane again, or ride Beau: She had a lump in her throat and a prick of tears behind her eyes. It had all happened too soon.

She blinked, not wanting her father to know how she felt. It wouldn't help him at all.

"When are we going?"

"At the end of the three weeks, to give your mother a chance to get strong again. She's much better and looking forward to our visit on Sunday. You and me first and then Hal and Louise, as they only allow two visitors at a time."

"I wish I could take Pearl with me," Mandy said forlornly. She'd be losing everything she knew and everyone she knew. Hensham was nearly two hundred miles away.

"That's another thing." Her father seemed to be choosing his words. He had scraped most of the dressing off his food and it lay in a pool at the side of his plate. "This way, we move from a very expensive house in the South of England to a far less expensive one in the Midlands. Even if I buy Hunt Cottage, there'll still be a lot of money left over from the sale."

He put down his knife and fork and took an apple out of the bowl and began to peel it, concentrating on it as if it were the most important thing in the world at the moment.

"You and Louise and Hal are all being uprooted and it isn't really fair to you. Modern life has a lot to answer for. Thirty years ago . . ."

He stopped talking, and Mandy, watching him, thought that he was looking back into a past that was very different to anything she knew. Things were safer then, her mother often said. When we were young . . .

"Your mother and I have been thinking."

He grinned at her.

"Don't look so worried. It's good news, not bad. At least, I hope it is."

"So?" Mandy couldn't think of anything to say.

"So each of you can have something very special when we move. It isn't going to affect either Hal's or Louise's chances of doing what they want. At present you want something to do with horses, and though you may change your mind it would be a good idea to learn more and learn it properly. There's plenty of room for Pearl, if that's what you really want."

"Pearl? Can she really come with us?"

"Her owner offered her to me some weeks ago, as you spend so much time with her. She was rescued by Miss Levy, who isn't very well herself these days. She has to go into hospital for an operation and she's been worrying about the little donkey."

A donkey of her own. Pearl would be a link with home. Home. Mandy thought about it. Suppose Midnight hated Pearl?

"Well?" her father was looking at her as if he thought his news had been unwelcome.

"I didn't believe it could happen." Mandy ran round the table and hugged him. "Dad, it's marvellous. But what are Hal and Louise taking with them?"

"Louise can turn one of the outbuildings into a studio and have it properly equipped; and Hal is getting a moped. I don't want him on a big bike yet. Don't tell him. It's another secret. I'm hoping he can have it when he gets his results and that it will also be a reward for good work."

"Can I go down and tell Jane and see how Lindsay is?"

"I don't see why not. Don't take your bike. I don't like you cycling at dusk on that narrow road. I'll come and collect you later on."

Mandy wanted to dance all the way to the stables, at the thought of having Pearl move with them, and having horses in their own fields. Then she thought of Jane, who had to sell up, and of Lindsay, and became more sober.

Jane was just finishing her own evening meal. Mandy had only one thought in her head.

"How's Lindsay?" she asked.

Jane poured boiling water on to instant coffee in the big mug which Mandy always had, and grinned.

"Lindsay's fine. You can come and look at her

in a minute. And I've had some news. You'll never guess."

"You've won the pools?"

"Not quite. I didn't tell you in case it didn't happen. I applied for a job as a stable manageress about two months ago. I'd given up all hope of hearing, but they rang tonight."

Jane's eyes glimmered with excitement.

"I've not only got the job, Mandy, but I can take Beau and Dart and Tempest with me and Damon's buying Lindsay. He was still here when the phone call came through. I only wish I could take you too."

"Where is it?" Mandy asked.

"It's in Sussex. A very big riding stables on the coast. They like their instructors to compete, and I'll be able to do much more show-jumping, as I won't have to worry about leaving the horses."

Mandy sighed. "I wish you were coming with us," she said.

"We've sold our house and got to be out in three weeks, and Dad's renting the Hunt Cottage in Hensham. It's next door to the Hunt Stables, so I'll still be able to ride. At least, I hope I will," she added, remembering that money might still be a problem. Jane's lessons were reasonably priced. Lessons in Hensham might cost a great deal more.

"There are horses at the cottage," Mandy said.

"And a most beautiful black stallion called Midnight Magic. He was a racehorse. A great jumper."

"Midnight Magic? Are you sure that's his name?" Jane asked.

"Quite sure. He's beautiful. He's coal black with glowing eyes and the most marvellous sheen on his coat."

Mandy forgot the dread she had felt when her father told her they were moving.

"Midnight Magic? You must be wrong, Mandy. He can't be still alive."

"He is," Mandy said. "I saw him."

Jane was looking at her with a frown.

"If Midnight Magic is still alive, he'd be fifty three, Mandy. It just isn't possible."

Mandy thought of Luke and his wife looking at one another. Of Kirstie saying that she was privileged, and that the horse went with the cottage and they'd never get rid of him.

She thought of the horse. She had seen him so clearly, had watched him flirt his tail and seen his mane lift in the wind. For a moment she felt fear, and then a small thrill of excitement. The horse had welcomed her. He knew they were coming to live there, and he was the guardian of the cottage.

She knew without being told that she must also keep his secret. Jane was thinking of her own good fortune, and when Mandy's father arrived to fetch her, they drank to the future in cocoa.

"Everything's going to be wonderful," Mandy said, trying to convince herself, as she climbed out of the car at the front door.

It wouldn't be nearly so strange with Pearl as a link with the past. Her own donkey. As much hers as Sim was. She couldn't believe it.

"Better, maybe, but life's never perfect." Her father yawned, and picked up the newspaper he hadn't had time to read and wandered towards his study.

"I wonder what is in store for us? I've as much as you to learn. I've never lived in the country before, and I can't spend my days doing nothing so I have to find out some way to make that place work."

"I hope we'll stay there," Mandy said. Any reservations about moving had, quite suddenly, gone. She felt that someone was pulling strings behind the scenes, making everything happen, and that it could only be good. The horses were waiting for her, and Midnight Magic, her dream horse, would welcome her when they arrived.

"Maybe. We have a year to find out. I've a feeling it may be a very eventful year for all of us, but it's a challenge I never thought I'd have."

He paused, with his hand on the handle of his study door.

"You know, Mandy, sometimes what seems like disaster turns out to be a gift from the gods, giving people a chance to start off down a new road, and find a new adventure."

That night Mandy dreamed of the black stallion, and rode him down a long winding lane, through mist hidden trees that rustled and threatened her. They were being chased by an evil creature that was hunting them down.

Every time the padding paws and panting breath menaced them, the easy stride lengthened, and she knew that she was part of the horse and he was part of her, and that the two of them together could outrun any danger.

Mandy woke and savoured her dream. It had been frightening and re-assuring at the same time. She couldn't wait to move to Hunt Cottage.

Six

August was wet, but September came with a smile. One Saturday morning Mandy woke to bright sun, blue skies and the faint sound of distant water rippling over rounded boulders.

She loved the cottage, and loved calling in on Luke and his wife, and being greeted like a friend, and given orange juice and lemonade as her right. She did not like her new school, where she felt alien. Louise loved it, and settled in fast, but she was in the sixth form, in her last year, and had much more confidence than Mandy.

There were more societies to join at this school and the Art master was impressed with her drawing. Louise, always busy, was beginning to have a very satisfying life and had little time for her younger sister.

Hal passed his A levels with three Bs, and was often out on his new moped. He was preparing to go away to college and life was exciting for him too.

Mandy worried about her mother, as nothing

seemed to give her any pleasure since she came out of hospital.

Mandy walked out into the yard and stood by the field gate. One of the mares came up to her and nuzzled her. Sim sat beside her.

Pearl was already in the far stable. She had been delivered by a Land Rover and trailer two nights before and Miss Holt had settled her in.

"Introduce her slowly to the mares, or they might kick her," the old lady said. She was a frequent visitor at the cottage, with permission to walk round the fields whenever she chose. Mandy began to look forward eagerly to her visits. Like Luke and Millie, she always had time to listen.

The sun went in and for a moment she thought she saw a black shadow move among the darkening trees. A small wind whispered. The cloud vanished, and there was nothing there but an empty field and the three mares and the foal. Or was there a distant movement where the water played with the banks?

Her father stood behind her. He spoke and Mandy jumped. She hadn't heard him come.

He put an arm round her shoulders.

"Feels odd, doesn't it?" he said. "As if we were here on holiday and one morning we'll all pack and go home." He sighed. "Only it isn't our home any more. We used to come to a place like this on holiday when I was a boy. Maybe that's why I feel it's only temporary. Why don't you call in at the stables and see if they can take you for lessons?"

The foal flipped up his hind legs and bolted round the field. He bucked, and then came to inspect them. He was so full of life. Mandy loved watching his mad time at dusk when he raced against his shadow and bucked and kicked around the field, his rocking horse tail wagging.

Then he suddenly lost all his confidence and rushed to his mother to suck.

"No," Mandy thought. "I can't go to the stables yet. I don't know any of them. It's bad enough having to go to a different school and get to know new people there. I can't manage anything more. And I haven't got Beau to care for any more. The horses there might be much more frisky than Jane's, and I'd make a fool of myself. They might make me jump and I don't want to. I want Beau and I want Jane. I want to go home, too."

Her father hadn't waited for an answer. He had gone indoors. Mandy followed him and went up to her room, taking Sim with her.

The little dog leaned against her, his head on her knee, comforting her with his small presence.

It was a long time before she picked herself up off the floor. She looked out of the window, at the bucking foal. Behind him stood a black shadow, watching quietly, and then it was gone.

The days passed but nothing seemed to change.

"How's Midnight?" Luke asked her one day when she called in from school. Mandy had never before realized how lonely you could be, in a family, or in a big class at school. Everybody seemed to be so busy that they took no notice of anyone else.

Luke and Millie and Miss Holt were her only comfort. They seemed to understand how she felt.

"He's gone," she said forlornly. "I haven't seen him since the day we arrived. I'm not really sure I saw him then. I keep hoping, almost glimpsing him, but when I look, he isn't there."

"He's there. He doesn't like change any more than people do. Nor do dogs. Remember when we moved here, Millie?"

His wife smiled at Mandy and passed her the new baked scones that were still hot and dripping with butter.

"I hated being here at first," she said, cuddling a minute kitten that tried to climb her leg. "I felt as if someone had unplugged me and put me away in a cupboard. We'd left all our friends behind. Everyone seemed suspicious of us. We didn't belong. We thought Luke would go on racing. But that last accident . . ."

"What happened?" Mandy asked.

"My horse fell. Not Midnight. He never put a hoof wrong. Big bay called Symphony. Belonged to a musician. Poor brute fell on me. Didn't do me much good. I was in the running for Champion jockey that year." He grinned at Mandy. "That's life. You start out in one direction and events shift you down a different road. You think 'if only'. Saddest words in the English language."

"Have another scone and don't listen to him," Millie said. "It's a long time ago and it's a good life now."

Mandy took the scone. She wished she hadn't asked about Luke's accident. It had stopped him riding for ever. It didn't help her fears at all.

Walking home, Mandy began to wonder if she would ever find enough courage to ride again.

Seven

Mandy was alone in the cottage when Luke drove the little horse van into the yard. Her father was at the far end of the big ten acre field, planting trees to act as a windbreak.

Hal had gone away to college. October brought gales and rain, and the fields were sodden. The field nearest the cottage was dry, but the mares and foal had to spend most of their time indoors. Pearl was often free in the yard and beginning to make friends with the mares, nosing at them over the stable doors.

Her mother had gone to visit Miss Holt who had promised her some of the old family recipes for jams and wines and chutney. Everyone seemed to have shifted into a new gear, except Mandy.

"I wanted to be here. Why can't I settle?" she asked herself. She heard the sound of a car and moved towards the door.

"Trouble," Luke said, as he climbed out of the Land Rover. "Where's that dog of yours?"

"Sim? He's indoors. Do you want him?"

"He's the last thing I want. Look, lass, I don't know how to say this, but we've a big problem. You see, when Kirstie was here we could bring the creatures to her, and she'd heal them. Now, there's nowhere."

"What creatures?"

Luke opened the back of the horse box and let down the ramp. Cowering as far from the light as he could get was the dirtiest and thinnest Shetland pony Mandy had ever seen.

"He's been starved, beaten and terrified," Luke said. "I bought him this morning. Daft, as nowhere to put him, but Kirstie suggested that he came here, as he would have done when she lived here. The end stable is empty. That was always kept for our rescuees."

"And when he's well?" Mandy asked.

"Aye. That's the rub. He'll need a home, and a good one. We always did find homes for them. Kirstie knows a lot of people. Now she's not here, it might be different. It's a long job, healing them, teaching them to trust people. He's never had reason to trust anyone and he doesn't trust me."

"So how do we get him into the stable?" Mandy asked, with memories of a horse that Jane had bought fighting every inch of the way, determined not to leave the box.

Luke shut the door of the horse box again and fastened it into place.

"That'll take care of itself," he said. "Come on, lass, let's be looking at that stable."

By mid-morning the floor was swept and laid deep with fresh straw. Luke fastened a haynet so that the little pony could reach it without being caught up in it. Outside, the shadows shifted, and the mares watched with interest from the pasture. The foal bucked and kicked, playing at being a strong stallion.

Mandy thought she saw a shadow in the gloom beneath the trees, but was not sure.

"We've earned a coffee," Luke said. "May I beg one, lass?"

"What about the pony?"

He opened the horse box again. The pony was a dimly seen shape against the back, in the dark, his eyes staring at them. Mandy had never seen such a miserable looking animal. There was a large abscess between his shoulder blades.

"Fistulous wither," Luke said. "That needs cleaning for a start. Somebody hit him hard with something that damaged him. Have to watch your hands, Mandy, and maybe your feet too. He's afraid of being punched and maybe of being kicked. He won't forget and might kick out in terror. Might just curl up and die of misery," he added.

"We leave him there and get coffee?"

Luke nodded.

"Just sit and watch," he said. "I don't think he'll fail us. Kirstie and I, we've done this often before. Nobody to trigger the wrong atmosphere. Just wait."

Mandy poured boiling water on to instant coffee that she had spooned into two brown earthenware mugs.

It was a grey day, the sky overcast, and a little breeze worried at the strands of straw at the edge of the horse box. There was movement in the yard. Mandy held her breath as Midnight Magic walked across to the box. She saw him, black and beautiful, his coat shining, his silken mane and tail gleaming as if they had just been brushed. He walked up the ramp and into the box, filling it.

A few minutes later he backed out again, the tiny Shetland, dwarfed against the thoroughbred, following him. It hesitated at the edge of the ramp, distrusting the downward slope. Midnight whickered.

The clouds parted, and a thin ray of sun lightened the black coat. Sunlight caught the dark eyes, and Mandy saw the gleam as Midnight turned his head. She held her breath. Luke was smiling, and he put a finger to his lips.

The pony stepped daintily, fearfully, down the slatted boards to the ground, where the big horse seemed to stand and encourage him. Midnight turned and walked into the stable and the little Shetland followed. For a moment Mandy saw the two side by side, and then the sun vanished, the shadows shifted and the Shetland was alone.

"He never fails us. My old beauty," Luke said. He walked out into the yard, crooning softly, hissing between his teeth, and, very gently, closed the lower door of the stable.

"Time, and talking. Healing food. Kirstie's magic mash. Kirstie will come and dress that abscess. He'll not want a vet near him, not yet. He's too afraid. You can feel his fear."

"Midnight's done this before?"

"Often and often." Luke was looking over the stable door, frowning.

"He's not real," Mandy said.

"Real?" Luke turned to look at her. "What is real? Now, or then? When I was a lad of twenty, winning races, sure the world was waiting for me and great things would happen to me, and life beckoned and I was fit and eager, that was real. It's still real. It happened. I remember, as if it were yesterday." He sighed.

Luke spoke softly, watching over the stable door, where the little animal cowered in the deep shade against the far wall and dared not come towards them. He didn't even try to tug at his net though he was so thin that he must have been almost starving.

"Talk to him daily, Mandy. Teach him to trust you, to want to be with you and then one day we can start healing his mind; that will take longer to heal than his body. Now let's think about that mash. Have to put it down for him and let him find it. We'll terrify him if we go too near."

Luke had brought the feed with him. Mandy watched him mix bran in a bucket and cover it with boiling water. He added a few drops of liquid from a tiny bottle, and covered the top of the bucket with a sack. He saw her looking at the phial.

"Kirstie's special magic remedy," he said. "Does wonders. She has some odd recipes for feeding and for healing, but my goodness, they work. That mash needs to stand; and then give it him little and often. He's more than half starved and to feed him too much would make him very ill. A bit of treacle now, just a taste. I'll come by every day to look at him."

Luke's voice was soft, barely above a murmur. He opened the lower door. The pony, shivering at the back of the stable, was watching them, but it made no move at all. Luke tipped some of the mash into the old manger.

"Stables were here when the Kennels were being built. The old equipment can't be beat, lass. No danger from bucket handles here. The little stone trough for water is older than the house. There was another house here, before the cottage was built."

Mandy had a sense of continuity, of time flowing past, of the same kind of people doing the same things in the same way, over and over, generation after generation.

There was a throb on the air as the little tractor her father had bought approached the yard. John Hunt switched off the engine.

"Luke. What brings you here?"

"A favour needed, squire. We took a liberty, your lass and I. Kirstie used to have horses and dogs here to heal. Sometimes to stay. A little Shetland, neglected and abused. He's in the stable now, in need of a haven. No money in it. Only trouble. But the lass can help him trust people and Kirstie and I'll be over daily to make sure he's healed."

Mandy watched her father go to the stable and look over the half door. The pony seemed to shrink ever further back into the shadows.

"Maybe a new occupation for you, Mandy. If he does get well, would you like to keep him? He'd be a companion for Pearl. We've room to spare."

Mandy wanted to jump and shout and to hug

her father, but the pony would have been frightened. Instead she smiled, and said very softly, "Yes, oh yes."

Late that night, she lay listening to the movements from below. The mares rustled the straw. She went to her window and looked out into the moonlit yard. Midnight was standing beneath the trees, whinnying softly, and the Shetland was answering, for all the world as if they were telling one another the story of their lives.

Back in bed she lay watching the slim new moon slide across the sky. She was sure that she now had a purpose to fulfill.

Sleep was slow in coming. She went to the window again and looked out into the night. A shadow moved across the field. A black head looked up at her, and she watched as Midnight walked slowly towards the sheltering trees, and vanished.

Eight

The Shetland pony had very little interest in life. He sheltered at the back of his stable, a forlorn little animal, his head hanging low. He took no notice when Mandy came in to change his straw or bring him food, or fresh water. He did not respond to her voice. Not even his ears moved. His eyes stared into a remote place, where no one could follow him. He was enduring feelings that no one could share.

He barely shifted his head when Mandy spoke. She longed to groom him, to sort the tangles of mane and tail, to clean the dust from his coat. He was so shabby. It hurt her to think that someone had ill treated him so much that life was a penance and not a joy.

He had reacted only once, when Mandy picked up a bamboo cane that her father had left against the door of the second stable. As she carried it past his open half door he whinnied in terror at the sight of the stick. Mandy instantly dropped it on the ground, and slid it carefully out of his sight. He was shivering but she dared not go into him. She knew that would only add to his fear.

It was three days before he ate some of the food she provided. He did not seem to understand what his haynet was for and ignored it. Luke came daily, but went away shaking his head. Kirstie Holt had a bad cold and was not able to visit. Mandy missed her common sense and knowledge.

A whole week passed before the pony began to eat with more interest, but he showed no sign of making friends with anyone.

The abscess was healing slowly, but the daily treatment was torment for the little animal and did nothing to make him trust humans. He had to be fastened so that he couldn't kick or bite.

The vet, when he first came to clean the abscess, had used a tranquillizer dart. There was no way, then, that the pony could be touched by human hands without tremendous stress.

Mandy had made friends with the girls who kept their ponies at the cottage. Diane and Polly and Sarah came every day to feed and exercise and groom. The evenings were friendly times, with talk and the stable sounds. The stamp of a hoof, a wild whinny of delight as each mare greeted her owner, the frisking of the foal.

Sometimes Mandy walked one or the other of the mares round the yard. It was Mandy the mares greeted in the morning. Silver, who belonged to Diane. Freya, who belonged to Polly, and Tara, with her foal Sabu, who was Sarah's.

Sim loved them all equally and solemnly followed Mandy on her rounds.

Sabu now wore a light head collar, and a tiny felt saddle, so that he would be used to having something on his back when it became time to teach him to be ridden.

One day Mandy would go to the stables and book some lessons. She was saving her pocket money and running errands, and also baby-sat sometimes for a young couple who lived at the end of the lane. It was near enough for her to be able to ring her mother if she needed help with the tiny baby.

Mandy called in just once at Hunt Stables. She stood in the yard, too shy to speak to anyone, and was daunted. This was nothing like Jane's tumbledown and friendly establishment. Here the stables were in blocks, the yard was surrounded by troughs of bright flowers, the posts and rails white painted.

The indoor and outdoor schools were for experts, not for schoolgirls who were only just learning to ride. Mandy had watched part of a lesson, and knew she could never face the instructor.

Four girls were riding, one of them an eight

year old with a flying pigtail and a terrified face. She clutched her reins, or the edge of her saddle, or the pony's mane. Mandy, watching, felt almost an ache. She knew exactly how the child felt.

"Susan, how often have I told you not to hang on like that." The voice was sharp, without sympathy, anger just under the surface. Mandy, sensitive to voices, felt a hard knot in the pit of her stomach. "Relax. Don't drag on the reins, for goodness' sake. Get your heels down . . . down, I said. For heaven's sake, girl, can't you do one thing right?"

Mandy knew there would be tears in the little girl's eyes. She was riding, red faced, silent, trying her hardest and nothing was going well.

Mandy went home feeling daunted and scared.

Maybe the girls would let her ride their ponies, though without instruction she'd never improve. Her need for horses was satisfied by the presence of the mares and her own pony and donkey. Lessons could wait.

The family seemed to have forgotten she had ever had riding lessons and she didn't remind them. She had a letter from Jane, now settling in to her new home.

"I hope you've found a new riding school and a good instructor," she wrote. "I'm looking forward to hearing from you. It's a bit lonely here, but I am getting to know people, and of course I have my own horses with me. Beau's a great consolation."

Mandy missed Beau more than she had believed possible. "If I hadn't moved, I'd be riding him now," she thought. Then she wondered if that were true. She loved helping with the ponies, but even when Diane offered her a ride, she found an excuse for not getting up on Silver's back. She was very happy to walk her round the lanes. But ride her? No. That was different.

She knew that each day that passed made it more difficult to start again, and she would be more out of practice. Her parents had no idea how she felt and she couldn't tell Luke or Kirstie. They would never understand. They had both been top riders.

She took the ponies out into the field each day, fed them, cleaned the stables, and put down new bedding. Their owners groomed them at night. She enjoyed getting up before the family, and savouring the morning stillness. Sometimes she was aware of a black shadow under the trees, but he seldom came forward. He was always there, and his presence helped her. He was a promise. One day, she would ride a real horse as she now rode Midnight in her dreams.

In dreams, nothing went wrong. Nobody ran out of a gate suddenly, no car revved and no lorry slammed on its air brakes. There was no sudden waft of wind to blow a paper bag across the path; no people yelling unexpectedly across the road to one another as she went by.

There was just herself and the horse, and the jumps he soared over so effortlessly, and the muted roar of a distant crowd.

Luke now visited Hunt Cottage daily, sometimes twice, to look at the little Shetland, who Mandy had named Kelpie. A kelpie was a Scottish spirit that often appeared in the shape of a horse.

Louise said a kelpie was a big horse, and travellers were afraid of it, but Mandy was sure it was a tiny spirit horse, just the right size for pixies, if they existed. She didn't want to look in the dictionary. She liked the name and didn't want to be proved wrong.

"He's anything but a Kelpie," Luke said. "I always imagine them as little and full of fun. He's little, all right, but full of woe. Not sure he's going to make it, lass. We've done our best, but maybe it's his time to go. Better place waiting for him, no doubt, and surely without any people."

"Lots of people think animals don't matter," Mandy said. "They laugh at them, or tease them and say they don't have feelings. Some of the children at school are cruel."

They were leaning on the stable door, talking softly. Behind them the late sun lay across the darkened field. The mares were in their stables, and only a rustle of straw betrayed their presence.

The light from the kitchen shone on to Kelpie's dull coat.

He showed no desire to come out of his stable, or to look at the world beyond the safe darkness. He allowed them to clean out the straw. He allowed them to put in fresh mash. He watched them with incurious eyes.

Even now, he only endured their presence. He never greeted them.

"He needs Kirstie," Luke said.

"Why doesn't Midnight help him?"

"He'll come at night. Not even he can teach Kelpie to trust people. Only to trust horses."

Luke walked across the yard towards the kitchen. Mandy followed him. Her mother would have coffee ready for them. She enjoyed Luke's visits. He smiled at Mandy, a gnome of a man with a bright shining face and eager eyes that must have looked the same long ago when he was a jockey.

"Do you miss racing, Luke?" Sally Hunt asked.

"Nothing like it," Luke said. "No use regretting, but the memories are always there. The first win." His eyes were alight with excitement, remembering. "You never forget that. The first jump. The first time you set the horse right, and soar over, flying through the air."

He sipped his coffee, and took a shortbread biscuit.

"I wish you could have seen Midnight, the first time he ever won. It was a hard race, with strong competition. At the last two fences we were neck and neck. And then over the last with wings in his hooves and all the power in the world still left in him while the other horse died on its feet."

His face was alive with remembered excitement.

"Jumping. There's nothing like it. You must learn to jump, Mandy. To love it."

He chewed thoughtfully.

"Soaring through the air, you and the horse together. It's ecstacy. Midnight flew." He sighed. "Better be getting off. Millie can't manage alone when it gets busy, but early evening's quiet out of season."

He was gone, moving lightly on his feet in spite of his bulk. Mandy went out to look at Kelpie. He too was afraid of the world. She spoke to him softly before she shut him in for the night.

"Don't be scared. Nobody here will hurt you."

There was a rustle in the straw, and he took a few steps towards her. She held her breath, but he backed away. She longed to go to him and put her arms around him, to soothe him, but he refused all contact and she knew she mustn't hurry with him. He needed time to learn to trust people. Nobody had ever given him any reason to do so before.

"When he comes to me of his own free will, I'll start my lessons again," Mandy promised herself. Luke had triggered her ambition, but he hadn't stilled the fear. "If the pony doesn't come, I won't."

It put the burden of decision on Fate and not on her, and she was sure the pony wouldn't move.

She held out a carrot.

"Come on then. It's time to brave the world. We've made you well. You aren't nearly so thin and your coat's beginning to shine." She hissed softly between her teeth, the way Luke hissed.

Slowly, the little pony walked across the stable towards the door. To her surprise, he came all the way. He looked at Mandy, and then, hesitantly, stretched out his head and took the carrot gently between his teeth. She touched his cheek, a feather light touch, hardly making contact, and he backed away.

She had a second carrot. She held it out. This time he came a little faster, took it as gently, and stood, while she brushed her finger down the side of his muzzle.

He shifted away from the door.

"If he can be brave, then I have to be brave,"

Mandy thought. The decision was out of her hands. She had made a promise to herself, and she had to keep it.

Next day she woke to a bright frosty morning. It was half-term and she had the whole day free. Her father was planning to turn the far fields into a landscaped garden, and was already up and working. Her mother was still in bed. Mandy had taken her up a breakfast tray. She still tired easily and had to rest.

Mandy heard the gate latch click as she finished her own breakfast. She planned to go to the stables.

Kirstie was walking towards her.

"I can't sleep these days and I need exercise. I suppose one day I'll get used to living in Harper's Keep," the old lady said. "I still miss my home. One room is so restricted. I mustn't grumble. Nobody made me go. Only common sense but sometimes I feel it's daft to be sensible at all."

Mandy could think of nothing but the ordeal to come.

"What I would really like is to saddle one of those mares and canter over the moors all day. Or have my whippets back and watch them run in the sunshine. We can never have what we really want and when we have it we don't appreciate it enough."

Kirstie laughed.

"There, child. I mustn't bore you with my woes. I hope your parents don't mind me calling. I've no desire to haunt you."

"We need you," Mandy said. "Kelpie wouldn't be better without your help. I'd no idea what to do with him. Come and see him."

She led the way across the yard.

Willow, who had been lying in a patch of sunlight, saw her mistress and ran to greet her, mewing and weaving around her legs. She followed them and jumped on to the half door, as Mandy opened the top. Sim, always wanting to be in on any act, followed. His bright eyes gleamed at Willow, who swished his tail. They had never made friends, but they tolerated one another.

The little grey cat leaped lightly down on to the straw. The pony dipped his head to stare at her, and then, as if he had known her all his life, nosed her, and made an odd whinny of delight.

"He's had a cat as a friend before," Kirstie said. "She'll help him recover. She's obviously been visiting him. When he trusts one creature, he'll learn that we can be trusted too."

Willow was weaving round the pony's legs, was mewing to him softly. She jumped to the edge of the manger and he followed her. He dipped his head and began to eat with fervour, enjoying his meal. He had rarely done more than pick at it before.

"The turning point," Kirstie said softly. "He'll make it now. I wasn't sure."

Mandy held out a carrot. The pony looked at it, and looked doubtfully at the figure behind her. Miss Holt moved away, and stood where she could see and Kelpie couldn't see her.

The pony walked to the door. He took the carrot, this time without hesitation, and stood for a second while Mandy's hand contacted his soft cheek. He moved back, and the cat jumped to lie across him, purring loudly.

"That's wonderful."

Kirstie's voice revealed her pleasure. She opened the stable door and walked in, speaking very softly, almost under her breath.

"Hey, my baby. My little one. Who's been hurting you then? You're safe here. Come, little one, come and talk to me."

The pony watched as the old lady walked towards him. His ears moved, and he huffed. She held half a carrot in her hand and he reached out and nibbled at it. She put a hand on his neck, and he flinched, and then lifted his head and looked at her.

A moment later she stood with both hands on his neck, one at each side, and gazed deep into his eyes as if willing him to trust her. The brown eyes stared back at her.

"No need for fear. You're with friends," she said. "Mandy, come into the box with me and stand beside him. Touch him, very gently, on his cheek. Make sure you don't make any movement towards that sore place. He'll think we want to dress it and that hurts him. Then he'll shy off or kick."

Mandy walked inside. The pony watched her but did not back away. She hissed under her breath, a soft whispering noise that reassured him and told the animal that she was not a threat and did not intend harm.

"He's so thin," Mandy said. "I thought he'd have begun to put on weight by now."

"That will cure as he begins to feel better. He's very stressed. A new place, with new people and he's not sure if he dare trust us. He won't digest properly until he settles down and feels secure. He's beginning to trust us. That's enough for now. We must take it slowly. It takes months with a frightened animal, not weeks. It's never any use being impatient. All that does is set him back."

She stroked his neck while she spoke. The pony rubbed his head against her shoulder, and she smiled, a vivid smile that made her look younger and pretty.

"That abscess is healing. I'll come down every day and dress it. Now he's eating we can give him treats when I do it, so that he associates the treatment with pleasure afterwards, and not pain. Hopefully he'll remember his reward and not why he had to have it."

She rubbed her hand along his flanks while she was talking, just a touch, without any pressure.

"We don't need the vet to do it any more. He won't fear me. He's a sensible little animal and once we prove to him that he's safe here, I think he'll turn into a charmer. What will we call him?"

"I've called him Kelpie," Mandy said. "He doesn't look much like it yet, does he? I always think of them as happy creatures."

"He will. Let's leave him in peace now."

Kirstie closed the lower stable door gently. The pony followed them and looked out towards the fields. Mandy turned her head. Midnight was watching them, from under the trees.

She felt a sudden rush of excitement.

"Kelpie can meet the mares soon." Kirstie smiled. "I wonder if he has ever been in a field, or was always kept in a dark stable? He might be afraid of the open at first. We must take it slowly."

She looked across to the shadow under the trees, almost as if she were asking the stallion for advice.

"Mandy, come with me to the stables. It's high time you started to ride again. I've asked Debbie if I can teach you. It will give me something to do with my time. Planning your lessons, watching you grow and learn will give me so much pleasure."

"She sounds as if she's pleading," Mandy thought. "Something I can do for her. I'd never thought of it that way. I wouldn't have that awful woman who shouted at the that poor little girl."

Kirstie was talking eagerly.

"It's as exciting when a pupil wins as when you win yourself. It's as agonizing sitting watching them perform. Willing them to do it right, willing the horse to jump and the rider to help him do it well. You try to put your skill into someone else's body. What about it, child?"

Mandy felt the familiar terror dry her mouth. Don't be so silly, she told herself. She had no choice now, anyway. She was committed. She'd made a promise to herself, and she had to keep it.

There would be an extra responsibility, as Kirstie would be expecting her to ride well, and she knew that she didn't. Also she would ride badly because fear didn't just go away. Horses knew when you were afraid and she would be on a horse she had never even met before.

If only Beau were here.

Nine

Kirstie led the way into the yard at the stables. The girls working there smiled at her as she passed. Everyone was busy. One girl wheeled a heaped wheelbarrow to the midden, another carried buckets of feed, a third was tipping water from a carrier into handleless buckets held by a support in each stable.

An older woman with a mass of dark curly hair was playing a hose on the leg of a big bay hunter.

"Trouble?" Kirstie Holt asked.

"He's lame. A bit of swelling. He was jumping yesterday, and I don't think he was really fit. He doesn't belong here. He's one of our livery horses. His owner had him out and brought him back last night and left him without even bedding him down."

"Debbie is always picking up the pieces when other people fail," Kirstie said. "This is Mandy. My new pupil."

"You don't know how lucky you are," Debbie said. "You're going to learn to look at horses in quite a different way. I wish Kirstie could teach some of my instructors her ways, but they do have their qualifications, and they think they know better."

She turned off the hose, and began to wind a bandage on the sound leg. Mandy looked at her, puzzled.

"I thought it was his other leg that was bad," she said.

"It is, but he'll be taking all his weight on this leg, so that needs support too. I have to be very careful putting the bandage on his wet leg, or it might shrink and that would mean worse trouble."

Debbie smiled at her.

"There's a great deal to learn. Kirstie has taught me so much. Enjoy your riding. We'll have you better than anyone in no time at all with such a teacher."

"One day," Kirstie said. "You, of all people, ought to know that nothing good is ever achieved in a hurry. There's lots of groundwork to put in before she can be trusted with the horse I have in mind for her."

Debbie laughed.

"She's in for an instructive time, anyway. Maybe one day she'll be able to pass on what you taught her. It might make life better for a lot of horses."

Debbie Lineham was older than Jane but had the same enthusiasm. She did not look at them as she spoke, as she had eyes only for the horse she was treating.

"I hope his owner appreciates all I'm doing. And his vet bill," she said. "He's a ride-at-the-weekend owner, and sometimes we don't even see him then. I think I'll have to put his weekly fees up. I do more for this horse than for some of my own, as he's always riding it hard and injuring it. Last time it was Monday morning sickness."

"What's that?" Mandy asked, admiring the deft hands that made bandaging seem so easy.

"He'd said he was going hunting, so we fed the horse up. Then he changed his mind. When he did take the poor animal out it began to blow and sweat and to refuse to move as it was getting so stiff. Being a fool, he forced it, and it went down and had to be brought home in a horse box. It took several weeks to get him fit again; we had to keep him warm, ration his feed, and then of course once he started work again it had to be in tiny stages, building up more each day."

She finished the first bandage and looked critically at her work.

"Needless to say the owner wasn't around to do that and he blamed us, not himself." She sighed and started on the second leg. "You can go off people. Which reminds me, what's going to happen to our rash purchase? It's weeks since I've seen you, Kirstie."

"Mandy's keeping him. I'm not sure we've done her a good turn, as he's going to be a lot of work, but she's started well."

"Did you tell Mandy how we came to buy him?" Debbie asked.

"I thought Luke bought him," Mandy said.

Debbie shook her head. "Luke carries them for us. Kirstie and I decided we need another riding pony here, for the smaller children. We couldn't see what we wanted. As we were leaving that pathetic little animal came into the ring and the bidding started. He was going for horse meat, though goodness knows there was no flesh on him. Kirstie bid more than the knacker without even stopping to think and there we were with a new pony, that looks as if it will never be any use to us. Then I had an idea, which is why you have him."

"You never know," Kirstie said. "We've been surprised before.

She reached out her hand and stroked the big hunter.

Debbie straightened up and sighed.

"Kirstie, there's a lesson in the school and one of the ponies may need your special first aid afterwards. Do you feel up to it? Mandy could help."

"It's what I had in mind," Kirstie said. "I looked at the rides booked in and who was riding before I came. I've seen this group before. They've been coming for almost a year, haven't they?"

"They have," Debbie said, sounding rather as if she wished they hadn't.

"Just a minute. Here comes one of the parents now. I need to watch the small boy. If he isn't kicked by a horse or bitten by a dog before he's much older, it won't be for want of trying." Debbie walked towards the car before the child could jump out.

One of the girls came across to lead the bay to his stable, and smiled at Mandy.

Debbie smiled at the occupants of the car that had driven in.

"Susan won't be long. Perhaps Jason would like to come with me and ride on our rocking horse?"

She held out a hand to the small boy who climbed out into the yard. He scowled at her, but went with her quietly. His mother let out a long sigh.

"Last week he chased a bantam cock and pulled a feather out of its tail and frightened a girl who was riding a horse in from the lane," she said. "He's a very difficult child."

Kirstie led the way towards the indoor school.

Mandy, walking beside her, wished that they hadn't come. Wished that the pony hadn't forced her to keep the promise she had made. The knot of worry was there, the fear of failure, the fear of falling.

The indoor school was much bigger than Jane's. Four girls were riding, among them the same little pigtailed child who had looked so frightened. She looked terrified now, clutching her saddle desperately with both hands as they trotted in line diagonally across the tan.

"Miss Holt. How nice to see you."

It was the same instructress.

"Do you mind if we watch?" the old lady asked.

"By all means." Mandy listened to the voice, knowing it was put on to impress.

There was a small section bordered by railings. Kirstie led the way through a little gate and Mandy followed her.

"Now, girls. Show our visitors how well you can ride. Susan, dear, just relax. Keep your horse quite still, while the others trot. No need to hold your saddle. Tansy won't bolt."

The fair girl who Mandy had seen before trotted round the school. She rode well, and Mandy was envious. Across the school, change the rein, said a voice that had no hint of the shrill scolding that Mandy had heard before.

Kirstie Holt was frowning as she looked at the

pigtailed child, who had just been told to trot down the centre of the school and then turn right. She couldn't adjust to the stride of her horse, and was bobbing up and down without any rhythm at all. She was gripping the edge of the saddle as if she were certain that she would fall off.

"That's it, for today, girls. You're all doing well," the sugary voice said. "I'll see you next week."

Kirstie Holt walked out onto the floor of the school.

"May we keep Tansy? I don't intend to have her ridden hard, but I'd like Mandy to start on her. We'll unsaddle and settle her afterwards. I only have about fifteen minutes to spare, so it can't be a long ride."

Mandy thought she might be able to stand fifteen minutes. It was impossible to be ambitious in such a short time.

Susan slid off the pony in an untidy heap, and ran out of the door. A grey horse stamped, and his rider checked him hastily.

Kirstie took the reins which had been left hanging, and stroked the pony gently, as she waited for the other girls and the instructor to leave the school.

"Oh dear," she said when they were alone. "There's something very wrong there. Has no-one ever told that child not to run out of the school and never to leave her horse with its reins dangling? Tansy might have tried to bolt and caught herself up in them. She's trembling, poor thing."

"Jane would never let anyone do that, but the little girl's scared," Mandy said. She took a very deep breath. "And so am I, since I fell off Beau."

It had been very hard to confess. She wondered what Miss Holt would say, and if she would despise her.

Kirstie looked at her, and nodded.

"I know. And Luke knows. We were sure there was something holding you back. We were afraid too, when we started. Only a fool never knows fear. We'll conquer it, you and I, but slowly. Right now we have a very important job to do. Never mind learning to ride. That can wait."

"A job?" Mandy was puzzled.

"Look at Tansy. She's had the most horrible hour in her life. She's had her mouth savaged by cruel hands hanging on to her reins. She's had a girl on her back who was as rigid as a piece of wood, and whose terror affected her mount. She's sweating and she's miserable."

Mandy looked at the pony. She was a pretty animal, her mane pale gold, her colour rich chestnut. She moved her hooves uneasily, anxious to be out of the school and into her quiet stable where nobody asked anything from her, and nobody gave her confusing instructions.

"We won't have a lesson at all today. This is far more important. I want you to sit on her back and walk her, gently. Nothing else at all. Talk to her, soothe her. Show her that all hands aren't rough. Very easy on the reins, just a feather touch. She needs to have her confidence restored."

Mandy walked towards the pony. She wondered if she would buck or shy or even bolt. Tansy's eyes were anxious, and she moved away from the approaching girl.

Mandy had never thought of a ride from the horse's viewpoint before, or the horse losing confidence.

The pony was easier to mount than Beau, as she was smaller. The saddle was uncomfortable, with too high a ridge in the centre. Maybe they could change that. Maybe she could buy her own saddle. Maybe she would be able to ride well one day.

"Feel her. Feel how she moves. Just sit, as easily as you can. Get to know every tiny shift in her rhythm. The length of her stride, and how she puts down her legs. Is she smooth, or jerky? Slow, or fast? Positive, or needing a great deal of help from her rider?"

Mandy had never thought of any of those things before, either.

"She needs someone totally relaxed on her back for a few minutes: not much more. We need to unwind her. She's far too tense. I'm putting a leading rein on her. Then she can gain confidence from me as well."

Mandy thought about the horse. She forgot her own fear, as she tried to sit easily in the saddle, to hold the reins lightly, to use her voice soothingly. The sensitive ears flicked back to listen.

"When we ride, we train the horse as well as ourselves," Kirstie said. "A bad rider teaches her mount bad habits. You're trying to develop your pony's hearing, her sight, and her willingness to answer your commands. Hard hands on the reins means hard mouthed horses. Hard kicks as aids mean that the horse won't answer to gentle pressure. It's why so many riding school horses are tricky to ride. They have so many novices on their backs, all riding differently."

Mandy had never thought about that before either. Jane hadn't explained.

Round the school, moving steadily, quietly, gathering confidence as they walked. She was sitting loosely, and felt the give and take from the horse's mouth, felt the shift of balance from leg to leg, adjusting herself in the saddle, feeling a new dimension that she hadn't realized existed before.

"Use your legs. Use your back. Use your voice. Use your hands. You need to exercise, Mandy, as a good rider is never stiff. In a few weeks' time you'll be doing those exercises on the horse's back on the lunge rein." Mandy thought she could feel Tansy relaxing.

"Whoa," Miss Holt said softly and Tansy stopped, neatly four square.

"She's happier now. Ride with your arms folded, Mandy. Get the feel of the saddle, and of your balance. Walk on," she added to Tansy, who moved obediently.

"Right turn. Do you remember? Look to the right, right leg at the girth. Left leg behind the girth. Feel your way with the right rein, don't pull, that's it, take it up again, and ease on the left rein. Good girl. Easy, wasn't it?"

Mandy was startled to find that it had been easy. That she had done as she was told almost without thinking, following that hypnotic voice.

"Don't forget to look where you are going when you change direction. Then your weight will be right. Think all the time of how your weight affects the horse. You can unbalance him so easily."

Kirstie removed the leading rein.

"There, that's long enough. Just walk on. Across the school and down the centre to the door, and dismount without frightening her. Let's see what you can do."

Tansy had settled to an easy stride, moving purposefully. Mandy remembered to face the way they were going, to change her weight, as they changed direction. She walked the little mare down the centre to the door. She dismounted, and patted her horse on the neck.

"Thank you, Tansy," she said and was rewarded by a soft muzzle being pushed against her hand.

"Very good." Kirstie was smiling. "Now we have the privilege of taking her to her stable, and making her comfortable for the rest of the day. Would you like to walk her, or shall I?"

"I'd like to, please," Mandy said, and took the reins. Tansy followed her, eager to be back in her stall. She was quiet as they unsaddled her and removed the bridle. Kirstie helped with the rug, and then they leaned on the half door, watching her tug at her haynet.

"Watch her eyes, Mandy. They tell you all you need to know. Did you notice them before you rode her?"

"She was bothered," Mandy said, not knowing how to describe the desperately anxious expression she had seen.

"And now?"

Mandy walked over to the mare and stroked her neck. Dark brown eyes turned to look at her.

"She's calm," she said.

"People often don't think about their horses, or how they feel. They just ride them. Ride them too hard and overface them. Put them away without walking them to cool them down gently." Kirstie sighed.

"They don't even know enough about it to teach," she said. "All they do is tell children to keep their heels down and sit up straight and be easy on the reins. They don't tell them how the horse feels, how he responds. Don't even tell them what dressage is about."

Mandy stared at her.

"Don't you know?"

Mandy shook her head.

"It's to teach your horse to be supple, and light and to move well. To listen, to pay attention. It's the basics for everything you can do afterwards, as if your horse has learned to love his work, to watch where he is going, to balance himself, and you to balance with him, then there's nothing that's impossible for you to do. Jump, or hunt, or hack. It needs concentration. It needs daily practice."

She closed the half door, and Tansy leaned out over it.

Mandy patted her.

"In the old days of cavalry there was a command I always loved," Miss Holt said, as they walked across the yard. "The men were told after exercise, 'Make much of your horses,' and each man gave his horse three pats in unison. A reward for work well done. I was very pleased to hear you thank your horse." She laughed. "I ought to pat you. You did that very well, and instead of an unhappy horse we have one that's content and at ease and has been allowed to relax after an unpleasant episode."

Later that day, as she bedded Kelpie down for the night, Mandy thought back to her ride. She hadn't felt frightened once they began to walk. She hadn't been asked to do anything difficult, or to show her paces.

She had had an odd feeling that Midnight had been walking beside her, giving Tansy confidence which passed on to her.

It was only when she was drifting off to sleep that the thought came into her head.

She had had a lesson. It was nothing like any other that she ever had before in her life, but she had learned so much from it. Next time she rode, she would try to think of her horse. She knew that while she worried about settling Tansy, she had forgotten her own fear.

Ten

Mandy's life settled into a new routine. She worked hard at her lessons. Her classmates were still unfriendly, but that ceased to be important to her. She had too exciting a life of her own, and barely noticed that the other children had little time for her outside school hours.

No one in her form shared her passion for horses. That she learned to keep secret. When she wrote her essays she was careful not to write too much about animals.

She loved the early mornings, and the deep dew. The knowledge that Midnight was there, in the paddock, watching over her. She enjoyed the work with the mares, and the foal, who now let her groom him, and pick up his feet and examine them, and happily accepted the small light saddle that sometimes replaced the felt one that he wore.

Three times a week she rushed from school to the Horse and Garter, where Millie had a hot drink and sandwiches ready. Then she changed into her riding clothes. Kirstie was always waiting, sitting at the big table in the kitchen, often with the kitten on her knee.

The last lesson of the day at the stables ended at five. Then there was a gap before evening lessons in the indoor school started at seven. Between six and seven Debbie always taught her own horses. Mandy stayed to watch, and Luke often came in before the end of the session and drove her and Kirstie home afterwards.

Jane had been a good rider, but Mandy realized that Debbie was exceptional. Jane had been a good teacher, but Kirstie was unique. She didn't seem to be teaching. She was always asking questions.

There was always a horse for Mandy to "settle down". There were three of them, depending on the day of the week. Tansy was her Wednesday horse, after the small pigtailed girl. Tansy was always in what Luke called "a bit of a lather", and sometimes, if the lesson had been very bad, Mandy found she needed to think herself into a soothing mood, so that the pony could relax before being bedded down for the night.

She was so busy worrying about the pony and settling her into a happier mood that she forgot to be afraid.

Her Monday horse was a grey mare. Shona was stolid. Her rider was good and she enjoyed her lessons. She was schooled over cavalletti, and had a very sweet and easy stride. On her back Mandy could forget fear. Kirstie asked nothing of her at all for over a month except that she walked the horse to cool it after its lesson, and sat deep in the saddle, balancing herself and learning how each horse moved.

The Friday horse was a bay gelding. Sultan had an imp of mischief in him, and a quicker, shorter pace. Even at the walk he was awkward, but Mandy did not ride him until she had had several weeks on the other two.

Sultan was a newcomer to the stables, bought at the sales some six months before. Debbie had to cure him of bad habits, some of which he still possessed. He was apt to toss his head, or refuse to walk on when told. Mandy had to work at him even to get him to move on his bad days.

By the first week in December she had settled to all three.

"Tell me about your horses," Kirstie said, one Wednesday evening. Mandy was sitting on Tansy without a saddle. A small blanket was strapped to the pony's back.

"Move with her. Go with her, feel her. Tell me about her. What kind of horse is she? Have you learned about her, Mandy? Learned what she needs from her rider?"

"She's not much confidence," Mandy said,

surprised at herself. "She's not sure of people, and she gets frightened when something happens that she's not used to. Then she tenses up and if you aren't careful she just might shy. She did shy with Susan one day. I think she's the wrong horse for Susan. Tansy needs somebody who understands horses and knows how to ride."

Mandy was thinking hard.

"She tenses up if you pull hard on the reins. And she hates being kicked hard, she needs just a very light touch to tell her what to do. Not legs that grip like a vice."

"Suppose Susan stopped her lessons with Meg and had half an hour with us? What would you do?"

"What you do with me. Stop her trying to do all the clever things and just get her used to sitting in the saddle; to feeling right. Or even to sitting on Tansy, while the horse stands quite still, and I tighten and loosen her girths, and you walk round the school."

"Meg's leaving at Christmas," Kirstie said. "I'll ask Debbie if Susan could join us. I think she'd be happier if she doesn't have to ride with a group. Also she's holding the group back."

Mandy thought about that. She walked Tansy down the centre of the school, turned her and halted her. She had done it without thinking, without any fear at all. She had forgotten that

Kirstie was old and she was young. They were just two people very concerned with horses, thinking about the same things, and discussing a problem.

"I think it would be a good idea," Mandy said. "I don't mind sharing my time with you. Susan needs to learn to trust her horse." She had been watching the end of the four o'clock lesson on Wednesdays. Meg's voice grew sharper throughout the hour, and her scolding more severe. Tansy was beginning to play up more each week, with little restless starts, and a great deal of head tossing and fidgeting. One week she gave a buck that almost unseated Susan as another rider came too close.

"Keep your distance," Meg said, her voice furious. Mandy, watching, began to think that Meg had as bad an effect on the horse as Susan did.

"It's not a good lesson for Susan," she said. "The other girls don't always do as they're told. The fair one shows off, and I think she rides too close to Susan on purpose. And when Meg gets angry, Susan gets worse and worse."

Mandy was rewarded by a vivid smile.

"Good girl. I can see you're beginning to think. Meg is a splendid rider, but an impatient teacher. Now what about Shona?" Shona was her Monday mare.

"Tansy's eight and Shona's twelve. She's been ridden all her life by people in riding schools. Tansy hasn't. Debbie said she bought her two years ago from a girl who grew too big for her, so she's only had one ride before. Shona is harder to ride in some ways, easier when you get to know her."

"Why is she harder to ride?"

"She needs much more encouragement. She's hard mouthed and you have to be really firm on the reins to get her to turn, and she needs a lot of leg aids. Tansy only needs a feather touch. I'd rather have Tansy on a long ride; she wouldn't be nearly such hard work. Shona's not nearly so sensitive to touch as Tansy. And she needs to see the whip, though you don't need to use it on her. I never feel afraid on Shona. She feels so safe. But she's too big for Susan."

Luke had just come into the school.

"I told you Kirstie was a good teacher," he said. "Most instructors just tell you to put your heels down, sit straight and go with the horse. They don't tell you what the horse is about. Or that you need to think hard about every horse you ride. They're all different. Now tell us about Sultan."

"Trot down the centre of the school," Kirstie said, very quietly.

Mandy rarely trotted the horses. She was

always soothing them, walking them, cooling them. She had never before trotted on a horse without a saddle. She didn't even stop to think. A word, and Tansy accelerated gently and smoothly. Mandy caught the rhythm. At the end of the school she turned right and eased into a walk.

"Would you have done that on Sultan?" Kirstie asked.

"Without a saddle? No. I'd have been too scared. He's a rough horse to ride, unless he's very tired. I don't think I'd like him at the start of the day. He tosses his head too much. He's brash. All fire and fury and feels as if he might bolt the second anything startles him. He . . . oh, I don't know. He just doesn't feel right. He doesn't feel like Tansy and Shona. They're much smoother."

"They've had years of schooling. Sultan hasn't. Debbie only lets experienced riders out on him. He needs a lot of work to make him more obedient and more sensible. That's what schooling a horse is really about."

"Would you like to learn to jump on any of these three horses?" Kirstie asked.

Mandy felt the familiar panic thrill in her throat. She hadn't realized it was still there, hidden, waiting to surface. She was happy to walk, even to trot occasionally, but she didn't want to be asked to make an effort. Not yet. She didn't want to jump at all.

She wanted to go on helping cool the horses, not riding as she had ridden with Jane. A quick movement, a sudden shy, and she'd be on the floor again.

"Did you ever jump with Jane?" Kirstie asked.

Mandy shook her head.

"No. I never felt ready and Jane didn't make me. I trotted and cantered, and did a little on the lunge rein, but I never felt really safe. I think I wasn't ready for Beau."

She hadn't known that then. She knew it now. Jane had pushed her on further than she wanted to go, and faster. She had felt delighted at the time. Now she wondered whether she would have been afraid if she had gone on riding the quieter horses, and not been thrown off.

"Beau could be a tricky horse to ride, because he spooked at things. Like white lines and white cars. That was when I fell off. Jane only let the very best of us ride him."

She stroked Tansy between the ears.

"Was that the only time you fell off?" Kirstie asked.

"Well, no, but I was never tossed on to concrete before," Mandy said. Then she remembered.

A sudden flash of memory that came from nowhere. It had happened when she was only eight. How could she have forgotten? She had been riding a chestnut pony. She was out with Jane, and three other children. They had ridden down a bridle path and come to a tree trunk that had fallen across the track.

It was only a tiny trunk, not more than a foot high, but it barred the way completely.

Jane's horse jumped it smoothly and neatly, just lifting himself off the ground. Mandy, not realizing what was about to happen, followed. Her pony, afraid of the log, but anxious to follow Jane's horse, soared in the air, far higher than the eighteen inches it needed to clear the obstacle. Mandy, clinging desperately to the mane, had been unseated, and leaned forward as the hard head came back, hitting her in the face.

She managed to regain saddle and stirrups again, but it was ages before her nose stopped bleeding. She hadn't cried. Jane thought her brave, but every time she mounted, for weeks after that, her inside knotted and she felt sick. She didn't tell anyone. She explained her bruised nose by saying she had bumped into a glass door, not realizing it was glass. She hadn't wanted to stop riding, but she most certainly didn't want to jump again.

As the years passed she forgot everything except the terror that overcame her when anyone suggested she jumped.

Luke and Kirstie were watching her.

"When I was eight," she said, and told them.

Kirstie nodded.

"It had to be something like that. You'd try and forget, and in some ways succeed, but the fear lies there, and until you take it out and look at it and face it, it won't go away." She eased herself out of her chair. "That's why I want you to gain confidence slowly. We aren't going to do anything unless you say you are ready. A tensed up worried rider is no good to any horse."

Mandy dismounted. Leading Tansy back to her stable she felt as if she had slipped into another gear. She was understanding things about horses that she had never thought about before. Jane had talked about the way they behaved, but not the character that affected the way they needed to be ridden. Riding lessons with Jane were just that. Learning how to hold the reins, to sit, to trot, to canter, but never thinking about what the horse was learning, or even if it did learn.

"I might as well have been riding a bicycle up to now," she thought. "That doesn't have feelings."

She checked the water bucket, and left Tansy tugging at her haynet, a contented little animal that rewarded her each time she put her away with a gentle push against her cheek that was almost a kiss. The little mare had pretty stable manners. She accepted a food reward with soft lips, and was the easiest horse of all to groom, loving the feel of the brush against her skin.

Sultan was ticklish and fidgeted constantly, so that those who groomed him had to avoid his hooves. He didn't mean to tread on anyone but he couldn't stand still at all. He made terrible toothy faces and grinned and gritted his teeth and shook his head.

Shona had to be shoved around, as she liked to lean against the wall and it was impossible to groom the side that was leaning.

"Enjoying yourself, Mandy?" Debbie asked, as she walked over to the stable to fetch her Arab stallion. Mandy thought him the most beautiful animal she had ever seen, except for Midnight.

Mandy nodded, as she closed the stable door and shot the bolt and fastened the padlock. Boys had opened the doors one night and let five horses free, as they had at Jane's. Debbie now took precautions.

"She's doing well," Kirstie said. "I think it's time."

Time for what?

Mandy looked at them, and Kirstie smiled.

"Time to reward you. You're learning well. You may not yet be on the road to winning a world class, but you're making a splendid start.

Knowing what riding is about, what you are about and what horses are about will take you anywhere. Though never fast. It's taken me a lot of my life to learn that, Mandy. I was always in a hurry when I was your age. When I was older, too. I hope you'll learn to make haste slowly at the beginning of your career and never forget."

"She's taught me not to hurry my horses," Debbie said. "You don't know how lucky you are."

She was leading the way across the yard to an alleyway that led to the back of the big house. Mandy had not known it existed. It led to another small row of stables.

Mandy looked at them, and then looked again, unbelieving. There, his head over the half door, was Midnight Magic himself, his eyes shining. She went over to him and put up a hand and touched his cheek. He was real, he was solid, he was warm, and he looked into her eyes with total confidence and trust.

She had to be dreaming.

She pinched herself hard on the wrist to make sure she was awake. The pinch hurt.

Luke and Kirstie and Debbie were all watching her.

"It's Midnight Magic. But how can he be? I don't understand," she said. "I don't believe it."

Eleven

Mandy was sure she was dreaming. She put out a hand and felt the muscled neck. The horse blew at her and his breath warmed her face.

"He is real, Mandy." Kirstie was laughing, her eyes alight with pleasure. "He's Midnight's great-great-grandson. I call him Star. He's the last foal I ever bred. He's seven years old, and he's destined for stardom. He has wings in his hooves and far more potential than Midnight."

Mandy had never known anything like the feeling that swept over her. She had never seen a horse that looked so magnificent, not even Midnight Magic himself, when he came to her in dreams. If only she could ride this horse.

"One day, you will ride him," Kirstie said, as if she had caught the thought. "Not yet. It takes four years to make a horse; it takes four minutes to ruin him. You need to learn to ride as if you were part of the horse. You need to learn horses. To think like a horse, to know instinctively just what it will do before it does it."

She sighed.

"Meanwhile Debbie is schooling him. I only wish I could. Memory isn't enough." She braced her shoulders, as if throwing off wild fancies.

"When will I ride him?" Mandy asked. She had no doubt that, one day, she would.

Kirstie looked at her, as if trying to see into her mind.

"When you've earned the right. You can look after him if you like. It means getting up every morning very early, before you go to school. Coming down here and mucking out; feeding him; grooming him. Getting him ready for the day. And after school, before you go home, then he's your charge too."

"I can do that?" Mandy couldn't believe her ears.

"Yes. But it has to be done every single day, without fail, weekends as well. I'm putting him in your charge. He's yours to ride one day, if you learn to care for him, and keep him in good condition; groom him till he shines. Know him, in the stable and in the yard. Learn him, Mandy."

"Can I start tomorrow?"

"Sure," Debbie said.

"Don't forget you also have Kelpie to look after, and the donkey. It isn't going to be easy, child."

* * *

Mandy couldn't wait for morning to come. She lay awake, listening to the owls calling. Hooves rustled the straw in the stables, and a cat yowled.

She was up as soon as the alarm rang, and out on her bicycle. The quiet streets were strangely empty, except for the early morning milkmen and the paper boys.

The stables were already alive though, with girls working hard at mucking out and feeding. Mandy had never realized they started so early, but there were over twenty horses and the first rides were at nine.

Star greeted her with a nose rubbed against her shoulder. She tied him to the ring at the back of the stable, carefully checking the knot. There was a big muck square outside, ready for her, and the fork and broom.

When she had swept the floor she found fresh straw ready for her, outside the door. Debbie put her head in, smiled her approval and went away again. By the time Star was groomed and fed, Mandy had to race home on her bicycle. Just time to care for Kelpie and Pearl and turn them out into the field, and clean their stables. Then it was time to change for school.

By then she knew that when she came to ride Star, she would indeed have earned the privilege.

She now came straight from school to the stables, where Kirstie was always waiting for her.

She continued to ride Tansy, or Shona, or Sultan, according to the day of the week.

Three horses. Three different feels to them. Three different strides. She was beginning to understand Sultan. He didn't pay attention; he lacked concentration and he was a plague of a horse on a windy day, breaking his stride with small double beats on the ground.

Mandy learned to know what he would do next and to anticipate, to balance herself, to use her voice to soothe him. "Don't be silly, it's only the wind, you big baby."

The wind blew round corners, screaming, and sounded against the corrugated iron roof. Mandy realized the horses would never know what made the odd noises. They must think there were strange animals there, perhaps waiting to catch them, and old instincts would arise. The need to bolt became paramount at times, and somehow had to be overcome.

On windy days her rides, even at the walk, were exciting. She prepared herself on the way home from school, thinking about the horse she was to settle that evening. Tansy disliked wind, but endured it. Shona might dance and toss her head when an extra hard gust screamed past the door.

Life was so busy. As soon as she finished her ride it was time to prepare Star for the night.

She began to learn a great deal about him. Pigeons nested in his stable and he loved the birds, and watched them fly in and out.

If he felt restless he dipped his head hard in his bowl and splashed water everywhere, making a sodden mess of his straw.

Sometimes he resented grooming and then would take a lock of Mandy's hair between his lips and tug. A gentle tug that said "Go easy. You're being too brash."

On frosty mornings he was irritable, not liking the cold. He watched his pluming breath with amazement. On windy mornings he was impossible, fidgeting from foot to foot and swishing his tail, so that, if she weren't careful, it caught Mandy across the face, stinging her.

She was always impatient to meet him, to be greeted affectionately, an affection that grew between the two of them daily.

Homework in the evenings kept her so busy that the days fled past. She could never understand girls at school who complained constantly that they were bored.

There was to be a Christmas party at the stables. The horses were to be dressed up and the riders to parade on them in fancy dress. The week before, Mandy arrived late, having had a puncture.

Susan was on her own, with Kirstie walking

Tansy round the school on a leading rein. It was Susan's first lesson with Kirstie. Meg had left, and there was a new instructress, but Susan had dropped out of that ride.

"Mandy. Would you watch us and tell me how Susan is sitting?"

Round the school again, across the top and down the middle.

"She can't sit properly," she said. "Tansy's too wide for her. Her legs are spread eagled and she hasn't any chance to balance herself. She's trying to grip with her legs, which she shouldn't be doing anyway."

"So she's never learned to ride as she's always had to hang on for dear life," Kirstie said. "Off you come, child, and Mandy will fetch another horse for you."

"A smaller horse? But there isn't one," Mandy said.

"Go and look in the stable next to Star."

Winter was beginning to bite. There was frost in the air and it was already dark. Lights shone over the stable doors and in the alleyway. There, next door to Star, who whinnied with pleasure when he saw her, was a tiny pony, saddled and ready for riding.

Debbie, busy with her stallion, looked out over his stable door.

"That's right, Mandy, take her."

Mandy checked the stirrups to make sure that they were up and didn't bang against the pony's sides. She led the little dapple grey down the alleyway and across the yard into the riding school.

"This is Posy," Kirstie said. "I bought her specially for little girls like you, Susan. Would you like to mount her? Talk to her first."

Mandy watched as the child went over to the pony. She whispered to her, and threw her arms around her neck. She was smiling as Mandy helped her mount.

"Lead her," Kirstie said, settling herself in the big chair that Debbie now kept in the school for her.

"Just sit comfortably," Mandy said. "Relax and feel proud as if you were riding in front of a huge audience. You've got the best horse in the world and you're the best rider in the world. Everyone's watching you. You know you're the greatest."

Susan pulled herself up in the saddle. Within minutes she was sitting well, and Kirstie nodded approvingly. As Mandy passed her the old lady made a signal. Mandy frowned, puzzled, and then realized Kirstie wanted her to remove the leading rein, but to keep close to the child.

She unclipped it, but walked as close as if it was still clipped.

As they passed Kirstie, the old lady reached out a hand and held Mandy, preventing her from moving. Susan walked on, alone, down the school, and turned right and then walked up the centre and halted her horse. She bowed, as if to a judge, the smile on her face almost splitting it.

"I can ride," she said, disbelief in her voice. "It's quite different on Posy. I feel safe. And it isn't such a long way to fall," she added.

Kirstie laughed.

"You aren't going to fall. Little girls make the place untidy if they lie on the floor. We can't have that. Debbie said you want to give up riding lessons. Do you want to now?"

"No. Oh no. That was fun. I wasn't a bit afraid. And nobody was cross with me. That makes me do everything wrong."

"You'll be riding with me in future," Kirstie said. "Time I picked up the reins again instead of thinking I'm too old."

She stood up as Luke came into the room.

"You and Susan can put Posy in her stable," she said. "Debbie will see to her. You still have to put Star to bed for the night."

"I can lead her," Susan said. "She's not big and frightening like Tansy."

"Tansy isn't frightening if you're the right size," Mandy said. She thought, as she helped Susan close the stable door, after unsaddling the little pony, that it would have been lovely to have a smaller sister.

She thought so even more two weeks later, watching Susan ride Posy down the school, and receive the prize for the best fancy dress. She had come as Cinderella, wearing a frilled dress that she had worn as a bridesmaid a few months before. With her hair loose, and her face alight with excitement she looked a different child. Her mother had made an enormous yellow extension to the saddle that looked like the top of a pumpkin.

Her smile grew even bigger when Kirstie gave her a red rosette marked *For Special Progress*. She held it up for Mandy to see as she passed.

"Not much fun in the early morning, is it?" Luke said, when Mandy called in on her way back from the stables in the dark and frost on Boxing day. "No time off with horses."

"He's worth it," Mandy said. "When do you think I'll be ready to ride him?"

"Depends on you, lass. You're coming on, but you haven't begun to jump yet. Kirstie is waiting for that."

"Is Star my carrot?" Mandy asked.

"Carrot?" Luke laughed. "No, lass. Kirstie doesn't think that way. She sets you challenges and if you take them and work with them and succeed, then she sets another."

"Challenges?"

Luke was frying bacon. Mandy, always desperately hungry after her morning work, could hardly speak for a watering mouth. He set down a full plate in front of her.

"Put that under your belt, lass. You look starved and I mean that the way we mean it in Lancashire, where it means blue with cold, not hungry. It's a rare raw morning. You need to cream those hands, or you'll end up in trouble."

Mandy's hands were sore. Mucking out was hard work and the cold didn't help. The icy wind had chapped them.

"Not all glamour, looking after horses. You get down to it and you put up with it. Challenges now. You've had several."

"Like what?"

" Getting up in the morning every day, week in, week out, winter and summer, and doing your own horses and then doing Star. Six in the morning day after day soon sorts out the men from the boys." He piled his own plate high with bacon and eggs and fried bread and sat down opposite her. "Kelpie. He was your first test. We wondered if you would take enough trouble to calm him down. Or be interested in such a sick and sorry mess of a pony. Or teach him to trust, to look after him."

He stopped talking to eat, and then continued.

"Kirstie didn't have a cold. She stayed away on purpose so that you had to do most of it alone. I just checked, not for your sake, for the pony's sake. We couldn't have him harmed by neglect because you weren't the right sort of girl."

Mandy laid down her knife and fork and stared at him.

"You bought the pony on purpose to test me?"

"That's right. Kirstie has waited for years to have some child she could teach everything she knew. A child that hadn't been marred too much by poor teaching from someone else. A child to groom for stardom. It had to be the right kind of child. A child who really cared about horses, not just about winning prizes." He filled his mouth and chewed thoughtfully. "Too many think of the glamour of it, not the work that goes on day after relentless day, keeping your horse fit, grooming him, cleaning his stable; cleaning tack; washing horse blankets; caring for him when he's sick and giving him time to recover. Understanding him."

Mandy picked up her knife and fork again. She wanted time to think.

"What was the next challenge?"

"Your three horses. A lot of girls would have thought that what you had to do was dull. They all want to get on and do the exciting things, not the things that a horse may need. Whether you would do as Kirstie told you; whether you would think about them and their different characters and the different way each needs to be handled. Tansy is easy; Shona can be tricky and frankly, I thought Sultan was a mistake and she was asking far too much of you."

"He scared me at first. He doesn't now. He's a big softie, and he plays up because *he's* a bit scared. Those wind noises in the school upset him badly. But he settles as soon as he knows I'm not scared by them."

"See what I mean?"

Mandy nodded. She was beginning to understand a great many things she hadn't understood before.

"Were there any more challenges?" she asked.

"Susan and Tansy. Kirstie knew the first day she saw the child ride that the horse was wrong for her. She wondered if you would recognize that. Meg didn't. Debbie never interfered with Meg's lessons so she didn't realize either. Took a long time to find the right pony as we needed one with sweet manners, one that had been schooled well, and that wouldn't scare poor Susan even more."

"And what's the next challenge?" Mandy asked.

"I think now you have to challenge yourself. You're learning all the time, but so far you haven't even tried to progress far enough to take your first jump. No use trying to ride a world class show jumper if you're scared, lass."

Mandy cycled home. She had a great deal to think about.

She borrowed Louise's handcream to rub into her hands, and then went into the big field. The mares came to greet her, to see if she had food for them, and the foal rested his head on her shoulder. These were tough little ponies, used only for hacking. The girls rode them but rarely schooled them.

They were easy to look after, even when their owners were unable to come, as they only needed a morning cleaning and feeding, and then could be out all day provided the weather wasn't too bad. She brought them in, as soon as she returned from school, to clean straw and their evening feed.

She always left Pearl until last. Pearl was a link in her life, part of the past and part of the future. The little donkey had gained in confidence too, and her eager bray always greeted Mandy whenever she came home.

She still told the donkey her secrets, while Sim watched, waiting patiently for his turn to be part of her life again.

"None of it is what I expected," she told Pearl,

as she groomed her. "It's all much more exciting."

She closed the last stable door, and threw Sim's ball for him. He hurtled into the twilight and returned to her, and she felt a growing excitement bubbling inside her as they went indoors.

Her parents were sitting in the big kitchen, Willow on her mother's lap. The excitement spilled over and Mandy smiled at them. Neither of them ever saw the black stallion, and she thought that sometimes they felt that she and Luke and Kirstie were playing some kind of game.

She felt closer to her parents than ever before. Hal and Louise, both on the brink of new lives, flew in and out of the house, never staying at home for long. Louise had the lead part in the school play. Hal, so briefly home for Christmas, was almost a stranger. He spent most of the time out, or filled the house with enormous friends whose booming laughs and long legs seemed to occupy all the available space. Then he was gone again.

Mandy wanted to tell her parents about the horses. She wanted to tell them about riding, but she knew they wouldn't understand.

Sim, wanting a biscuit, suddenly sat and begged. Mandy laughed at him, and tossed it to him to catch.

"I do love it here," she said, knowing the words were inadequate.

"It's odd, isn't it?" her father said. "It's the best thing that has ever happened to any of us, and yet, at first, it seemed as if it was the worst." Mandy knew exactly what he meant.

Later that evening Mandy stood at her bedroom window with Sim beside her, his paws on the low sill. She looked down the paddock. Midnight stood there in the shadows beneath the trees. He was watching her intently as if telling her it was time to move on. The future waited and unless she took the next step, it would wait for ever.

Twelve

The weeks fled past. Mandy woke early, washed, dressed, ate a slice of toast with her coffee, and then raced off to the stables. Cold days and wet days were a penance that she learned to endure. Luke was right. No glamour, just hard unremitting work.

She wished she could greet each day with as much excitement as Sim. He couldn't wait for her to open the door, and, no matter what the weather, he charged into the morning, full of joy at being alive. His eager presence helped Mandy through the morning chores.

There was no time now for big breakfasts with Luke. Her mother always had hot food waiting for her, though, and as soon as she had eaten it, it was time to set off for school.

The days passed fast.

At the beginning of February Mandy was given a new horse to settle. Misty was piebald, black and white, with a look in her eyes that told of mischief. Debbie bought her to replace a twenty five year old chestnut that had been retired to a rest home for horses.

Misty appeared to think that her role in life was to disconcert humans, and, if possible, to upset them completely, though not to the extent of throwing them off.

The piebald mare saw ghosts in the school. There were several there as far as she was concerned and they lurked in corners, or down the centre, just where a rider stopped to salute the judge.

It was there she saw her first apparition with Mandy on her back. Mandy trotted to the centre and prepared to halt. Misty spooked, twisted in the air, and landed facing the door. There she stood and trembled.

Something awful in the middle of the floor. Mandy could see nothing whatever to alarm any horse.

"She does that," Kirstie said. "Trot her round the school and settle her."

Misty trotted happily until she reached the doors. This time the ghost was apparently in the cracks. She eyed them, tossing her head, and though Mandy was prepared by the tensing muscles she was not quick enough to stop the mare spinning round. Misty stood still, her sides heaving.

"You're daft," Mandy said, stroking the damp

neck. "What gets into you? There's nothing there."

There wasn't, next time, and for a few minutes Mandy trotted round the school, performed two twenty-metre circles, and slowed to a walk across the diagonal. She was totally unprepared when she passed a hard hat that had been left lying on the table beyond the rails that separated the spectators from the floor. Misty had previously ignored that. This time she glanced in that direction and took fright again.

Mandy, taken by surprise, lost her stirrups, gripped the mane and settled herself. Up the centre, down the side, passing the table again, visible beyond the rails, preparing for the spook. Misty walked on, with an air that said, caught you that time, didn't I?

Misty was Mandy's Tuesday horse, and Tuesdays became a day when anything might happen. She soon learned that her voice could prevent a sudden bounce into the air, or a half-buck, as if the little mare was determined to play up and then changed her mind, settling into an awkward movement that was very uncomfortable.

Whatever bothered her was never in the same place twice. One day it might start in one corner, and she would pass two more corners and panic at the fourth. She would ignore the table for four lessons and decide it was about to leap on her and kill her in the fifth.

Mandy removed any whips or hats that were there, but one afternoon Misty decided that the table itself was dangerous and tried to bolt. Mandy persuaded her that that was absurd, but suffered during the process as she felt uneasy for the rest of the ride.

"She's impossible," Mandy said.

"She needs understanding," Kirstie said. "You're managing her very well. I know she isn't easy."

Everything was wrong with the mare's transitions. At first Mandy thought she was to blame, but she discovered that though she could make the other horses move smoothly from the walk to the trot, and back to the walk again, there was no way she could do so with Misty.

The piebald only had one desire and that was to jerk. She changed pace in a way that Mandy found impossible to describe.

"She's just downright awkward in every way," she said, after one particularly exasperating afternoon when the school appeared to be peopled with bogeymen.

"I do everything I do with the others; sit tall, close my legs to try to balance her. She won't respond. She's so ungainly. I keep my hands light; she just doesn't answer, and then, just as I begin to wonder what I'm doing wrong, she seems to think, "Oh well, maybe I'd better do as she wants," and she catches me out, and I nearly come off. Goodness knows what makes her spook. I just can't make her out at all."

"She's typical of a riding school horse that has never had proper training," Kirstie said. "If you can master her, she'll teach you far more than a horse that has already been trained. Just ride on."

She watched as Mandy turned up the school and rode down the centre towards the door, where Misty had bucked before.

"No need to be silly," Mandy said, as they approached. She turned to the right, and walked back towards Kirstie who was watching intently.

"You have to help make Misty. I think the spooking's just a silly game that she's been allowed to get away with. We have to cure her. Talk to her more. She liked that."

Misty's walk was the most uncomfortable that Mandy had ever met. She dragged her hindlegs; she tossed her head, she appeared to have no idea what any of Mandy's commands meant. On Tuesday nights Mandy was always glad to get home and bath and ease the aches from her body.

She supposed that Misty was yet another challenge, just as the stable work with Star had been. Kirstie had very odd ideas about teaching.

Somehow the settling down had turned into

lessons and horses were often waiting for her, having not been used on the afternoon rides.

She did whatever Kirstie asked, never realizing that gradually she was working far more with each than ever before. Almost everything was done at the walk. Misty, circling, began to improve.

She moved far more easily and was less jerky. At first, she had been very stiff, and rarely paid attention.

By the beginning of April, when cold nights were rare, and the daffodils were dead memories in the flowerbeds, Sultan was trotting over poles. Never more than three, or he became wildly excited.

One evening in May, when she went to Star's stable, she found it empty. She stared at the open door, a feeling of desolation overwhelming her. Nobody ever took him out when she was due.

There was nothing to do but go and watch the last lesson. Someone must be riding Star. Debbie was busy with her Arab stallion, so it couldn't be her. Mandy felt a rush of jealousy. Star was her horse. Nobody else had a right to him.

Then she reminded herself that that was silly. Star belonged to the stables, to Kirstie, not to her. She now knew that Kirstie had chosen Debbie as she had chosen Mandy's own family for Hunt Cottage. The horses needed someone who loved them, and did not only want them to use as moneymakers. Debbie paid what in effect was a large rent, and when Kirstie died, she would inherit everything, as the old lady had no family of her own.

Mandy walked into the school, expecting to find that the four o'clock ride had just started, and they were using Star because another horse was lame. She didn't want to watch someone else riding him.

There was nobody but Kirstie there. Star was tied to a ring beside her, and the old lady was talking to him. He watched her, and listened, and then, hearing Mandy's footsteps, turned towards her and whinnied.

Kirstie watched with a smile as the wise head nosed deep into Mandy's pockets and Star found his treats. He rewarded her with a mouth against her ear. She laid her cheek against his nose.

"We're going into the outdoor school," Kirstie said. "Up you go."

Mandy had groomed Star for months. She had cleaned out his stable and put in fresh bedding. She had fed him. She had led him. But she had never before been on his back. Now she rode out of the great double doors as if she were dreaming, not believing that at last all her wishes had come true.

She watched the bunched muscles in his

shoulders ripple as he walked. He was power, he was energy, he was magnificent and he moved as if he were flowing along, so effortlessly that Mandy felt as if all she had to do was sit still and let him take her where he would at whatever pace he chose. None of the other horses she had ever ridden moved like this.

The reins were an extension of her arms. He talked to her through them, telling her he felt good, telling her he was enjoying himself, telling her he was looking forward to showing her what he could do. His ears flickered, listening for her voice, or pointing as something caught his attention.

He was so easy to read.

She couldn't believe any horse could move so smoothly after some of her battles with her weekday animals.

Kirstie was smiling.

"Well?"

Mandy thought. Kirstie never expected an immediate answer. The questions always had an inner meaning.

"If you'd let me ride him before, I'd never have known how good he is," Mandy said. "The other horses taught me."

Kirstie's expression rewarded her.

"Now you know what I wanted you to learn. How do you feel?"

"As if I've come home."

Luke was walking towards them, with Debbie beside him. His face reminded Mandy of an old and mischievous cherub. He was grinning widely. Two of the girls stopped their work and watched as Mandy put Star through his paces in the school.

The horse eased from the trot to the walk and back to the trot without the least hesitation, the movement so fluid that Mandy found it hard to believe.

There were trotting poles at the edge of the arena and she took him over them. He stepped daintily, watching his stride, correcting himself once when she was too eager, and her untimely command caused him to falter. When the movement was finished, he turned his head to look at her as if to ask why she had interfered.

She looked at the little hurdle. That hadn't been there yesterday. She trotted round the ring, delighting in his movements, enjoying herself as she had never done before. Fear had vanished. There was only supreme confidence. On this horse she could do anything.

They were not alone in the arena. There was another horse in front of them, a black stallion, his mane flying. Midnight Magic had come to lead his great-great-grandson. He floated in front of them towards the hurdle. He was over it, effortlessly. It was such a little jump, his body said.

Star followed him. They were gliding towards the jump. This wasn't riding. This was a new dimension. Star took the initiative and before she had realized it they were over, the movement so subtle that she couldn't believe it had happened.

She turned her horse, marvelling. A touch on the reins, a shift of her weight, a suggestion from her legs and he was obedient to her at once. They approached the jump from the other side. How could she ever have been afraid of such a tiny obstacle?

Again Midnight was in front of them, leading them, showing how eay it was, how little there was to fear. She was balanced, she couldn't fall, she knew what to do without being told. She would show all of them that she was ready to start the real learning now.

She knew she had met Kirstie's challenges and passed with honours.

She trotted round the school, and halted opposite Luke and Debbie and Kirstie. She bowed as if she had just completed the most complex set of jumps in the world. Her eyes were shining, her cheeks were glowing and she sat as proudly as any champion rider.

She could never tell anyone of the excitement she felt, of the total satisfaction, of her own delight in overcoming her fears. Then, looking at Debbie and Luke and Kirstie, she knew that they understood. The first time, Luke had said. There's nothing like the first time. There would be many more, but this she would remember for the rest of her life.

She patted Star firmly three times on the side of his neck. Make much of your horses. Kirstie smiled at her, pride in her own eyes.

"I told you she was a teacher in a million," Luke said. Mandy knew he was wrong. Kirstie was unique.

She didn't move. She wanted to savour the moment, to fix it in her mind for always. She looked about her, needing an entire picture, one that would be there when she was as old as Kirstie and unable to ride.

There were woods at the edge of the mown grass, the trees rustling in a soft wind. A bantam cock strutted at the edge of the outdoor arena. Debbie's ginger cat was washing himself by the green water butt beside the back door of the house.

Above her was blue sky, marbled with a hint of cloud. The sun was westering, challenging the blue with floods of scarlet. Sleek heads looked out over the stable doors. There was a background noise of voices; of clanking buckets, and of laughter.

A pigeon flew over and Star looked up, as if recognizing the bird. There was a flicker of movement beneath the trees. Midnight was poised in the shadows, watching them, his eyes brilliant. Luke and Kirstie turned towards him, and then looked at one another and smiled.

As Mandy watched, the black stallion leaped the paddock fence and was gone. She was not at all sure that she hadn't dreamed him.

"Our hero. He always comes for great occasions," Kirstie whispered. So they had seen him too. A great occasion? Then she knew. Her first ride on Star. She had a sense of other such occasions, waiting in the wings, in the far future.

She dismounted and led Midnight's great-great-grandson back to his stable. As she unsaddled him and rubbed him down and groomed him, she knew, without any doubt, that the two of them would, one day, form a partnership that the world of showjumping would never forget. Kirstie would teach her as no other girl was taught now.

It was hard to say goodnight to Star. She wanted to stay with him. She was impatient to ride him again. She wished she need never be parted from him. She put her arms around his neck and hugged him.

He dipped into her pocket. There was nothing left and he nipped her arm very gently to tell her he was displeased, and that, great horse though he might be, he could still be mischievous and she had better watch out.

Nothing was as easy as it looked.

He stamped an impatient hoof as she closed the door. It was hard to believe the afternoon events had happened.

She stood outside, listening to his movements. He had walked over to his haynet, and she knew he would be tugging at it, forgetting completely about her.

Tomorrow she would be thirteen. Tomorrow she would begin building on what she had learned today.

That night Mandy dreamed of riding. The horse she was riding was Star. He was a gleaming hero, his satin coat shining under bright lights, and she and he together were clearing every obstacle on a course that was bounded by barricades and clapping crowds.

Higher and higher they jumped until they were flying, and the Earth was small beneath them and the future waited for her to fulfil her dreams.

Outside in the meadow a black stallion walked beneath the moon, and left no footsteps in the dew.

LIONS · TRACKS

Suffer Dogs

Frank Willmott

The bottom of Eric's life fell out when his mother told him he was to go and live in Baverton with his Aunt Ruby. Money had always been scarce since Eric's father left home. But Baverton was a million miles away. He'd have to start from scratch – new town, new school, new friends. And he'd never set eyes on Aunt Ruby. His fears are unfounded. His life surges ahead, and a few surprises lie in store for him on the way.

LIONS · TRACKS

Centre Line

Joyce Sweeney

Moving, frank and funny, this is a powerful first novel about a group of teenagers, the five Cunnigan brothers. Their mother died ten years ago and their hard-drinking father either beats or ignores them. They decide to cut loose and leave home.

The exhilaration of freedom, feasting on junk food and picking up girls is soon tempered by dwindling cash, fear of police capture, and the danger of their small group splitting up.

Abrasive and real, *Centre Line* is a story of survival.

All these books are available at your local bookshop or newsagent, or can be ordered from the publisher. To order direct from the publishers just tick the title you want and fill in the form below:

Name _____

Address _____

_____

Send to: Collins Childrens Cash Sales
          PO Box 11
          Falmouth
          Cornwall
          TR10 9EN

Please enclose a cheque or postal order or debit my Visa/Access –

   Credit card no:

   Expiry date:

   Signature:

– to the value of the cover price plus:

UK: 80p for the first book and 20p per copy for each additional book ordered to a maximum charge of £2.00.

BFPO: 80p for the first book and 20p per copy for each additional book.

Overseas and Eire: £1.50 for the first book, £1.00 for the second book. Thereafter 30p per book.

Armada reserve the right to show new retail prices on covers which may differ from those previously advertised in the text or elswhere.

ARMADA